Praise for

The Red Dog Conspiracy

"Beautifully written."
— GABRIEL CLASON

"... complex characters in a dangerous world."
— GENEVIEVE DODD

"Do yourself a favor and read this .... You will enjoy."
— GERALD CHAMBERS

"... a breath-taking chase through the brilliantly blended world that the author created."
— HEIDI ANGELL

"... definitely worth the read for those who love a good mystery."
— UNCAGED BOOK REVIEWS

"The author creates vivid scenes and complex characters and a plot that keeps you turning the pages."
— COLLEEN MOONEY

"I honestly can say that I need the next installment immediately."
— FICTIVE DAYDREAM

For more reviews,
Visit JacqOfSpades.com

BOOKS BY PATRICIA LOOFBOURROW

FICTION

RED DOG CONSPIRACY

Prequel: **The Alcatraz Coup**

Part 1: *The Jacq of Spades*

Part 2: *The Queen of Diamonds*

NON-FICTION

Edible Landscaping on $1 A Day (Or Less!)

THE ALCATRAZ COUP

A Prequel to the Red Dog Conspiracy

Patricia Loofbourrow

To those who fight for their right to live.

The undisciplined man does not corrupt himself alone:
he sets the whole world afire. — Rumi

September 17th

Acevedo Spadros stood before his Bridges History class, chalk in hand, bemused at his students' fidgeting. *The last bit of the hour on the last hour of the day must feel interminable.*

"We've talked about the geo-political situation which led to the formation of the Kerr Alliance long enough." He grinned. "Now let's discuss something you care about: the founding of the city. In 1500, Inventor Benjamin Kerr completed the dome and chartered Bridges as an independent city-state with the North American Federal Oversight Committee."

The class murmured, some in confusion.

Acevedo smiled. They hadn't read the chapter. "That was the original name of the Merca Federal Union."

The ones who had read the chapter leaned back smugly, the rest had "oh" faces, recognition dawning as to the vast span of time and how it changed things.

Acevedo loved seeing that look on a child's face; it was the best part of being a teacher. "Those of you who **read** chapter four: any questions?"

A dozen hands shot up.

Acevedo pointed to Jack Alcatraz, a boy of seventeen with curly brown hair.

"How did they build the dome?"

Acevedo chuckled. "Best ask your chemistry or physics teacher that. It's made of graphene, I think."

The class laughed, but it was a good laughter, fond and relaxed.

Acevedo walked to the map of Bridges: a circle, cut into four equal Quadrants by their four rivers, a relatively small island at the meeting of the rivers in the center. "The Inventor King was a deeply devout man. He laid the city out like a bridge board —"

The class murmured in confusion.

"— to him, the rivers represented the Holy Cards. He felt the rivers were the real beauty and wealth of the city, the knowledge and life they held flowing to its center. He laid out the city focused on the rivers, not the land."

A chorus of "oh."

Acevedo smiled. "When Inventor Kerr built Bridges, the only inhabited part was Market Center." Acevedo pointed to the island in the center of the map. "But he made it defensible. When they were building the city in the 1400's, they faced attacks by the surrounding tribesmen until they could raise the dome. In time of need, they were able to retreat to the island." He pointed to the four bridges in turn. "The island's only accessible by the bridges from each quadrant. With the way it's elevated," thirty-foot sheer cliffs above the water, "plus the Suction, it's an effective defense."

"Like a moat!" Jack said.

Acevedo preferred for children to wait to be called on. "Yes."

Jack didn't seem finished with his questions. "Why is the Suction there?"

Why doesn't he know this already? Acevedo glanced around. Every eye was on him. *They're really interested.* "The water is sucked down from around the island's base and pumped under the rivers. Then the water is returned to the rivers at the waterfalls around the Rim." He went to the board and drew a cross-section of the river pump mechanism and the path a river's water might take.

More "ohs," and Acevedo felt surprised. "You didn't know this?"

"No," several children said.

Acevedo felt uneasy. *What else haven't they been taught?*

He needed to get the class back on track. "The important part is that Benjamin Kerr built it. He also created a political situation unseen since the Catastrophe, which has given us peace for almost 300 years: the hereditary monarchy. The Inventor King believed that the benevolent hereditary monarchy was, and I quote: 'the most perfect form of government.' With that in mind, turn to page forty-seven."

Acevedo picked up the textbook on his desk. A bookmark lay within it, and he waited for the students to find the page. "We're not going to go down this list right now, but I want you to study the overview of the Inventor King's treatise on governmental decorum tonight. Anyone else have a question about the founding of the city?"

Molly slowly put her hand up. Since her father had died, she looked exhausted. "When did they build the fence?"

The other students glanced away, embarrassed.

Acevedo let out a breath. *I hoped not to have to talk about this so soon.* Every year he had angry parents in to see him after that discussion. "It was much later. About forty years ago. If we have time near the end of the year we'll get to it."

She nodded, not meeting his eye.

The bell rang.

"All right then," Acevedo said, as the students packed up their books and papers. "Chapter five for tonight. Please write down any questions and turn them in at the start of class. I'll see you and your parents later today for conference. If you can't make it, or need a different time, tell me now."

No one came to the desk, so Acevedo erased the board. The students filed out, laughing, jostling, and teasing as they went, leaving the door open.

Acevedo straightened his desk, swept the room, wound the grandfather clock in the corner, and set up a few chairs beside his desk. The first parents would arrive soon.

He put the files of the students scheduled for today's conferences on a chair to his right beside his desk as a maid came in. "Tea for you, sir?"

"Yes, thank you."

The woman curtsied, put the tray on the counter, poured him a cup, then set it before him on a saucer. "Will there be anything else?"

"No, thank you. It's conference day, so I'll be in late. You can go; I'll lock up."

"Thank you, sir." She curtsied and left.

Acevedo drank his tea as he skimmed the student files. Molly was the only one he had any real concern about; he felt glad her mother had time to see him.

A soft knock at the open door, but it startled him. Jack stood in the doorway with a tall, clean-shaven man in his late thirties, hair and eyes dark brown like Jack's.

The man looked familiar.

Recognition dawned. "Xavier? Xavier Alcatraz?"

Acevedo went to shake Xavier's hand. Fondness surged in him as he did so, and Acevedo enveloped the man in a tight hug, then pulled away, grasping the man's upper arms.

The short, chubby boy was now a sturdy man, taller

than he was. "It is you! Dear gods, how you've grown! I didn't recognize you."

Jack stood there gaping.

His father smiled at him. "Mr. Spadros was my favorite teacher in high school." Xavier turned to Acevedo. "You were everyone's favorite teacher in high school."

Acevedo laughed. "You're too kind." He gestured to the chairs. "Please, sit." They did so. "I hope you've been well?"

Xavier Alcatraz nodded. "Very well." He seemed astonished. "Last month I was appointed head of the Guard."

Acevedo stared, mouth open. "You've done very well indeed!" He stood, leaning over to shake Xavier's hand. "Congratulations, sir."

Jack beamed at his father.

Acevedo sat. "Jack's done a fine job in my class. Reads his work, always ready with questions. High marks. I don't have any complaints." He smiled at Jack's blush and spoke to the boy. "Do you have any future plans?"

"I'd like to become a surgeon, sir," Jack said. "When my mother became so ill, the physicians were kind." He shook his head, eyes downcast. "Her case was hopeless; all of them said so. But the surgeon was the only one who seemed to **do** anything for her."

"My word," Acevedo said to Xavier, chagrined. "I'm so sorry for your loss, sir."

Xavier gave a fake smile. "It was long ago."

Jack spoke over his father's last words. "I'm good with my hands and not afraid of blood." He straightened. "Dr. Royal Diamond of Diamond Surgery Associates has agreed to apprentice me."

Acevedo, never having heard such a name before, glanced at Xavier in confusion.

"A reputable fellow," Xavier said. "I've checked his

credentials. Over in the Northeast Quadrant. His shop is small, but many other surgeons have trained with him and speak highly of his work."

"So Jack Alcatraz is to become a surgeon," Acevedo said to Xavier. Then he turned to Jack. "Well, my boy, you could do much worse than that. I hope you'll remember that the history of a thing is what creates the thing itself."

Jack nodded, his face thoughtful; Acevedo could see the gears turning. Then the boy smiled. "You're right! I shall be careful to learn the history of each malady I encounter, to understand how it was made."

"Very good," Acevedo said, encouraged. "Then I have helped you." He glanced at the clock. "My next family should be here soon." He stood, as did they, and shook hands with them both. "Stop by again soon," he said to Xavier. "You're most welcome."

Xavier nodded. "Perhaps you'd like to come for dinner?"

Jack seemed a bundle of enthusiasm at the thought.

"Why, of course," Acevedo said. "Any time you wish."

Molly and her mother, a fine-figured woman with black hair dressed in deep mourning, stood in the doorway.

Xavier glanced back, then turned round to bow to them. "My apologies, madam. Come, Jack." They walked past, Xavier nodding to Molly's mother as they left.

"It was good to see you both," Acevedo called after them. Then he went to Molly's mother. "Acevedo Spadros, at your service." He took the woman's black-gloved hand and kissed it.

Her eyes were warm and blue. "Katherine Bluff, sir. A pleasure to meet you."

"Please, come in." Acevedo gestured to the seats, and they all sat. He opened Molly's file, not quite knowing where to begin. "I'm grieved at the recent loss of your husband."

She made a graceful motion, almost as if she curtsied in her chair; he couldn't have described it any other way. "Thank you kindly, sir."

For a moment, Acevedo was at a loss for words. "Um, I can see it's caused a great deal of strain for Molly." He put his hand down to open Molly's file, and realized it already lay open. "She seems often tired, and her grades have suffered."

Molly flushed red.

"I don't mean to berate you, dear; I feel concerned for your welfare. How may I help?"

Katherine said, "Your kind words are all the assistance I fear you can give." She put her hand on her daughter's. "Our financial situation is precarious, and Molly has had to work evenings to help."

Acevedo gaped at Katherine. A young, well-bred girl, working? She still grieved her father's death! "What work?"

"I care for children in families without servants," Molly said, "when their parents wish to go out on the town. I have motherless children I care for when their father must work late. Cook their dinner, feed them, put them to bed. I do my reading when the children are asleep." She hesitated. "The nights I don't get children, I sweep at the grocery down the street. That doesn't pay as well, but no one bothers me."

Out in a public place, at night? "My dear, you must leave this grocery at once. It's dangerous, not to mention improper for a girl of your standing."

Molly said, "But —"

"I insist. You may come after school every afternoon and sweep for me: I'll pay you whatever the grocery pays per hour, plus ten percent."

"You're too kind," Katherine said. "We couldn't possibly impose upon you like this."

"It's not an imposition at all," Acevedo said. "It frees me from sweeping, plus it ensures the rest and safety of my student. She's a bright young lady, and I don't wish her grades to suffer any more than they have." He smiled. "So you see, it's beneficial for us both."

Katherine gazed at Acevedo. "I see now why your students love you so."

Flustered, Acevedo said, "Thank you." His cheeks burned as he glanced at the clock. "I'm afraid our time is over; my next family will arrive soon." He rose, as did they, and took Katherine's hand. *Those beautiful eyes.* "It's good to have met you." Then he turned to Molly. "Until tomorrow."

In truth, he had five minutes until the next family arrived, but Acevedo sat at his desk, head in his hands, a desperate need for some time to collect himself. *This is a student's mother, and a recent widow. What am I thinking?*

He took a deep breath, let it out. At least he could help keep Katherine's daughter safe, and if anything was to be, it would come in time.

***

Xavier Alcatraz walked home with his son, the boy excitedly chattering about dinner with his teacher as horses and carriages went past. "I didn't know you had Mr. Spadros as a teacher, Dad."

"Oh, yes," Xavier said. His former teacher was much older now, but had the same enthusiasm for his students. "Back then he had to fight to allow young ladies to study alongside young men. That's where I met your mother."

Xavier smiled to himself at the memory of his wife as a young girl. It didn't hurt so much anymore. "Now it's considered normal."

"I don't understand people who say we should go back to the old ways," Jack said. "It seems wrong not to let girls go to school too."

A sleek new steam automobile chugged past.

"There are always people who say we should go back to the old ways, Jack. That's why you learn history. The old ways weren't as great as some make them out to be."

When they got home, his fifteen-year-old daughter Joy met them at the door. "How much trouble is he in?"

Xavier laughed. "He got a good report."

"I made enchiladas," she said, and he could smell them. "They're almost ready."

He hugged his little girl, kissed her wavy brown hair.

Not his little girl, his young woman. He needed to arrange her debut soon. "I appreciate it."

After dinner, Xavier sat with the newspaper on his front porch. The news wasn't very good these days. The recession was worse, the gang violence was worse, and another grain shipment was hijacked. Xavier hoped none of his men had been injured this time.

The Guard is stretched too thin, Xavier thought. But he understood the situation: hungry people would do whatever they could to eat.

Thank the gods for the Dealers. If the holy women hadn't built their aid stations outside the fence, there would be rioting by now.

He was refolding the newspaper, about to get ready for work, when Blocker came by: a short, wiry guy with white-blond hair. Xavier didn't know the man's real name, but he came around about once a week.

"Hey," Blocker said, "how are you?"

They had guys like this around since he was a boy. "Good, how about you?"

"What can I get you?"

Xavier recalled his father's words: *You always want these*

guys to help you. You never know when you might really need them, and these aren't guys you want unhappy with you.

He thought about Joy. "I do have something you can help me with. My girl's turning sixteen this summer."

Blocker grinned as if he hit the jackpot. "Her debut! I'll get right on it. I know several fine establishments which can help you."

Blocker began listing off dressmakers, meeting halls, stationery shops, never actually naming names — just "a friend I know" where he could "get you a good price."

For which he's going to take a cut.

If Xavier thought about it too long, it rankled. But guys like Blocker — and more importantly, the gang or crime family they belonged to — didn't like it if you went to these establishments yourself. "Get me something to show her."

"Of course — you got a fine lady in making. Even educated." He nodded. "Ought to have lots of suitors. I can scout around for some good ones if you want. Any interest in getting her into a Family?"

Those thugs shooting up the streets out by the fence? "I'd rather stick with gentlemen. But thank you for the offer."

"Whatever you want, Mr. Alcatraz. But mark my words, one day these Families are gonna **be** gentlemen."

Uneducated criminals? Hardly. "Thanks for your help, Blocker. I need to get ready for work."

As Xavier Alcatraz got into his uniform and tucked his children into bed, he thought about his talk with Mr. Spadros earlier. *I'm the luckiest man alive. Two beautiful kids, a great job.* He sat next to his son. "I'm very proud of you."

Jack gave a shy one-shoulder shrug.

"No, I really am. I know it's been hard on you since Mom died. But you've been a great brother to Joy, and ... " Suddenly he choked up. *My son wants to be a surgeon!*

Jack grabbed his hand. "It's okay, Dad. It wasn't your fault. And me and Joy, we're doing fine. Really, we are. Don't worry about us." He grinned. "You better go, or you'll be late."

Xavier hugged his son then, hard. "I love you."

"I love you too, Dad."

***

After a long day at school and meeting with so many families, it felt good to be home.

Acevedo opened the door, and Scoop came to greet him, tail wagging. Good smells filled the air, and Acevedo's stomach rumbled. He called out in Italian, "I'm home."

"About time," his uncle answered from the other room. "Icicles formed on your dinner."

"Hush your mouth, Vincenzo," his mother snapped, also from the other room. "You're not too big for me to spank."

Acevedo laughed softly as he came into the kitchen.

His father sat at the table reading the evening paper. The headline read:

DA: "RAMPANT CORRUPTION"

Royal Family Implicated

His mother set down her rag, wiped her hands on her apron, and kissed him on both cheeks. "How did it go?"

"Just fine, Mama. I have good students this year."

"You have good students every year," his father said. "It's because they have a good teacher." He peered at Acevedo over his spectacles. "Look at you. Positively glowing. Did you finally meet a girl?"

Was it that obvious? "Papa —" Acevedo began.

"Don't 'Papa' me, you little scamp. Sit down and eat. We can talk about her later."

Acevedo sat, and his mother put a plate of ravioli down.

11

Despite what Vincenzo said, it was steaming hot.

His mother sat beside him. "So what's she like?"

"Let the man eat, Nina," Papa said. "He just got home. Give him a moment's peace."

"It's all right, Papa," Acevedo said. "I met with one of my students' mothers, a recent widow. She's comely, that's all."

"Well, at least it's a girl you're after," Vincenzo said. "Was wondering about you there for a while."

Acevedo about spit out his food. "Really. Really? I don't see you dating anyone, Uncle Vinny."

Vincenzo leaned back. "All in good time." He took out a pipe, filled it from a pouch in his pocket, lit it. "You ... you're what? Fifty now?"

"Forty-five," Acevedo said. Despite being his uncle, Vinny was only a few years older. They had had this conversation many times. Acevedo stabbed at a ravioli. "Just never met anyone before."

"Forty-five. And here your dear mother and father sit, waiting for grandchildren."

Acevedo sighed. The topic used to enrage him; now he just felt weary. "You have twenty-four grandchildren, with six on the way. You need more?"

"Well, you are our eldest, dear," Mama said. "Your brothers and sisters have worried for you."

Acevedo snorted. "All in good time. If it's good enough for Uncle Vinny, it's good enough for me." He grinned. That should silence them.

They ate for a while, his family chatting about the news, the races, but Acevedo's mind drifted to Katherine Bluff.

Papa put down the paper. "So tell us about her."

They just wouldn't let it go. "She's ... I don't know, forty? Black hair, blue eyes —" He stopped as both his parents began nodding. "I just met the woman. And she just lost her husband. And her daughter is in my class. Please, let it go."

He mopped the sauce on his plate with his bread. "I won't be going with you to the opera next month."

Mama looked stricken. "Why not?"

"The woman's daughter was working in a grocery. At night. I gave her a job. I won't have money for the ticket this month. I'm sorry."

He didn't much like the opera, but his mother did, and they went every month. "I'll save up enough for next month, I promise."

Papa peered at him. "I think we can loan you the money, son. You did a good thing. I'm proud of you."

Uncle Vinny laughed. "You'd have all the money you need if you'd work for me, instead of that lousy school."

It was an elite private school. But opera tickets were expensive. "I'm not getting involved in your schemes," Acevedo said. "That's final."

Vincenzo puffed on his pipe. "People need things, I get them things. Nothing wrong with that."

"I'm not having this conversation," Acevedo said, putting his napkin on the table. Uncle Vinny was a criminal. *Why did Papa let him stay here?* "Thanks for dinner, Mama." He rose. "I've got some things to take care of." He went to Mama and Papa, kissed them.

"You're going to your room?" Mama said. "You just got home."

Yes, I'm going to my room. It's the only place I can find some peace. "It's been a long day." He smiled at her. "Dinner was great. I'll see you in the morning."

"But Acevedo —"

Papa put his hand on her arm. "Hush, Nina, let him be. Good night, son."

"Good night." Acevedo went to his room and closed the

door. A lamp by the door burned low, and he turned it up, illuminating the room.

For forty-five years, he'd lived in this room.

Maps covered the walls and tomes of military history in several languages filled the bookshelves — including the one he bought last week, which took up most of his paycheck. A large oval table in the middle of the room held that book, a map, and figurines depicting the Battle of Broadway: 1271 AC, when the Federal Army fought the Southwestern Tribes after they stormed the Serenity Valley construction site and killed everyone there.

They had great strategists on both sides, Acevedo thought.

The Wild Men weren't as wild as everyone believed. They just didn't want life under a dome.

He leaned his hands on the edge of the table, stared at the map. He was doing what he loved. He had a good life. He could do anything, go anywhere he wanted.

So why did he feel trapped all of a sudden?

It's that damn Uncle Vinny. The man was a thief. He extorted people, smuggled contraband into the city ... and the men he worked with were even worse. But Papa wouldn't lift a finger against him.

I can see not wanting to abandon your little brother, or turn him in, but one day Uncle Vinny's going to get us all killed.

Acevedo threw himself on his bed, thinking of Katherine Bluff. Her eyes, the feel of her hand in his. The graceful way she moved.

The school year had just begun. It would be wrong to court a woman whose husband just died, whose daughter was in his class. But in nine months?

He smiled.

This room of his had been a good little dome, but he realized he didn't want a life here anymore. If Katherine

Bluff would have him, life outside would be well worth it.

****

Xavier stood at attention next to the King in his white-paneled throne room, as he had for the last nine years. Xavier's job didn't entail much more than that, but it gave him time to think.

King Taylor Kerr, a thin, white-haired man with penetrating grey eyes, sat on his gilt throne listening to the night court. Each night, judges from all over the city came to get the King's ruling on difficult matters.

Xavier felt in awe of the old man: he could listen to a situation which seemed impossible, then calmly propose just the right solution. During court, the King wore his robes, but not his crown — which was for state functions only.

As usual, King Taylor's sour-faced son Polansky also sat in the hall. Polansky Kerr was in his early sixties, also white-haired. The man spent most of his days perfecting his hot air balloons at the zeppelin station up in the Northeast Quadrant. But every night, he was back.

When the last of the judges left, that's when Polansky began. "Half the cases tonight were merely symptoms of the moral decay in this city."

King Taylor leaned his elbow on the arm of his throne. "Why do you say that?"

"If we banned women from employment, there would twice as many jobs for the men. If we barred girls from school, there would be half as many schools needed. Save money on education, increase jobs."

"And have uneducated women? How would they be able to teach their sons? Or help their husbands with business? And how would widows survive if they had no employment?"

"They have families to support them. Or they can go

outside the fence with the rest of the derelicts."

"You're wrong, Polansky. We can't have half the population illiterate. That goes against everything the Inventor King —"

"Fuck the Inventor King! You want to quote nonsense from 300 years ago, go right ahead. We've become immoral, decadent. Women running around in loose dresses out in public, showing their faces, painted like whores. Gangs and crime families tearing up the city. We need order here —"

"We have problems, Polansky, yes. But not the problems you want to focus on." The old man shook his head slowly. "My father caused a lot of financial problems during his reign that we're still dealing with. But I have faith —"

Polansky yelled. "Bah! You and your faith in people. People are animals, and when I'm king —"

"Which I hope never happens —"

"Hah! What will you do, cut me down like a dog?"

Taylor Kerr peered at his son. "I've had advisers tell me I should have had it done when you were a boy."

"You're going to regret saying that," Polansky Kerr growled, then stormed out.

Every night was the same, but this was one of the uglier ones. That was the worst part of the job, pretending not to hear as the son shouted at his father. They seemed to disagree about every aspect of life in Bridges.

You're here to protect the Royal Family, not to judge them, he thought, not for the first time. Yet seeing Mr. Spadros again made Xavier remember the Inventor King and his rules on governmental discourse.

King Taylor went wearily to his room. The other three guards followed Xavier and the King. Two stood guard outside the royal bed-chambers while Xavier and his second, Fritz Zepik stood guard inside. They alternated through a short rest break while the ancient King was changed into his nightclothes by his manservants and helped into bed.

Xavier stood listening to the old man snore until he and his men were relieved by the morning shift. Rumor said there were secret passages into every room in the palace that not even the Guard knew about, and they were vigilant should someone come to attack the King in his sleep. It had never happened, but Throne Guards in the royal bedchambers was a tradition which stretched back 300 years.

The King usually woke before the morning shift arrived at 0400. At the end of the night, Xavier's back hurt and his legs ached as he went to his office to finish his paperwork. But his position held great honor, and there was no better-paying job available.

It was a good life. He was there for breakfast and dinner with his children, which was what really mattered. Soon Jack would go to his surgery apprenticeship, and Joy would begin receiving suitors.

Perhaps once the children are gone from the house, I'll move to training the guards. He wouldn't need the money as much, and it would get him off his feet all the time.

As he drove his steam automobile over the golden bridge to his house past the early morning horse-and-carriage delivery traffic to the island, Xavier considered what Jack said about people romanticizing the old days. Xavier thought of the editorials about "mismanagement": constant price fluctuations, intermittent food shortages, the potholes. Many people were just a few paychecks away from ending up outside the fence.

The King seemed like an intelligent man; why wasn't he doing something?

This new corruption scandal — the District Attorney claimed the King himself was involved. How could that be?

The finest food, hundreds of servants ... could a man his age really want more?

Then Xavier considered the son.

The thought of Prince Polansky Kerr becoming King someday frightened him.

September 26th

Acevedo stood in front of Molly's tall, narrow house and knocked on the door. No answer.

Molly had come in every day after school and cleaned while Acevedo graded papers, read questions the students submitted, and planned the next day's class. Her grades had improved, and she seemed less tired in class.

But she hadn't been to school for two days. Today was Saturday, and this was the address in her file.

He went to the window; the house was empty.

"Who are you?" An old lady stood on the porch next to him, grasping a broom as if to hit him with it.

He turned to the woman and bowed. "My apologies, madam. I'm Acevedo Spadros, Molly Bluff's teacher."

"Well, they were evicted the other night."

Acevedo stared at the woman. "Where did they go?"

"What business is that of mine?"

"You're their neighbor! Her husband just died! Could you not give them a room until they repaid their debts?"

"Damn poor people — let her go outside the fence with the other freeloaders." The woman turned and went inside; the lock clicked.

Acevedo stared at her door, shocked. *What's happening to this city?*

***

Acevedo didn't want to believe Katherine Bluff was taken outside, so he asked at the hotel, the hospital, yet found no trace of them. Finally, he had no other choice. He went to the main road out of his quadrant, to the gate in the black wrought-iron fence encircling the city.

The gate stood shut, rough-looking men loitering near it on the other side. Other rough-looking men stood on this side as if they guarded the gate; one came to his window.

"What's your business out there?"

"I'm looking for a widow woman with a seventeen-year-old daughter who's disappeared. Has she come this way?"

The man sneered. "Were they pretty? I might be able to find you ones like them — for a price."

"Have you seen them or not?"

"What business is it of yours?"

Acevedo remembered Uncle Vinny. "They owe me money. Maybe I should get it from you instead."

"Hold on now, I did happen to see the two you mention." He gestured to a pack of unsavory looking men who stood nearby. "Keep 'em back if they charge you."

Acevedo parked his steam automobile off to the side of the road as the men opened the huge wrought-iron gates.

Acevedo had never been to the fence before, and it both fascinated and repelled him.

The bars were as thick as his thumb.

No one charged, and the guard turned to close the gate behind him. "We don't open this after dark — if you aren't back by then, you're on your own."

Acevedo didn't plan to leave until he found Molly and Katherine. He grabbed the man's arm. "You're coming too."

"Hey now!" The man's friends beat Acevedo back, pushed him to the ground, slammed the gate shut.

Acevedo jumped to his feet, furious. "Where is she? You said you saw them!"

"They're in there, I saw them." He turned away, the group breaking into laughter.

There was no use for it. Acevedo set off, wary people

staring back at him.

***

After many hours walking through the tent city talking to dirty, sullen people, Acevedo felt exhausted. No one seemed to know where Katherine and Molly were.

He sat on a box, dispirited, while small children played in the dust nearby. One peered up at him. "You're not looking the right way."

This was odd. "What do you mean?"

"You don't ask where someone is that way."

"What's the right way to ask?"

"You say who you are and why you want them."

"I don't understand."

An old man sitting on a box a few paces beyond the children said, "We don't know you. You might be a cop."

Acevedo pondered this, then nodded. "My name is Acevedo Spadros. I'm a history teacher. Molly is a student in my class. Her father just died." Did he dare say it? "I met her mother a few weeks ago ..." Heat rushed to his face at the memory of her eyes; the thought of her in this awful place made him angry. "I need to find her."

The old man smiled at Acevedo's last words. "Ahhh. Now I know who you are." He pointed to the child who spoke earlier. "Tell the Bluffs a friend has come."

The boy skipped away from the fence, past the tents, and was gone.

Acevedo's heart began to pound. Would he bring them **here**? What would the old man tell Katherine?

Twenty minutes later, the boy returned. "Come on."

Acevedo followed the child past makeshift tents, open cooking fires, dirty children playing. The days were getting chilly, and no one had enough to wear. "How long have you lived here?"

The boy shrugged. "Always."

This boy couldn't be more than eight. How long had they been putting **children** outside the city? "How do you live? What do you eat?"

He shrugged, looking away. "Whatever the Dealers bring us. The trash trucks come all the time, but the food's not as good."

The boy turned away from the gate and went past sight of it. Then they crossed the main road from Market Center to the countryside. Ramshackle huts stood in the distance, but they turned left and went to a small lean-to. Inside, Katherine and Molly sat on a blanket, trying to cook over an open fire.

"Mr. Spadros!" Katherine sounded mortified. "I never thought to see you here."

"Molly didn't come to school," Acevedo said, feeling at once that this wasn't a good enough reason. *She'll know at once why I'm here.*

"I fear I have little to give you," Katherine said. "I had to sell most of my belongings to get this humble abode." She took a battered teapot off the coals, then smiled to herself. "However, I do have tea."

Acevedo sat on the blanket beside Molly. "I would be glad to take tea with you."

***

When his grandson came back, the old man got up off the box and told the children, "Let's go see your Papa."

The old man went past the tents to a building made of corrugated metal panels. The door stood open; his nephews Shuli and Wànzi stood guard outside.

His oldest son Crispin sat at a workbench facing the doorway, a lamp casting light upon his work. A thin man, he had long straight black hair and a mustache to match.

Crispin glanced up. "Hey, Pops."

"There's an insider here. Looking for his lady friend, he says, that new widow woman and her daughter. I thought you should know."

***

Crispin Hartmann nodded. "Hey, Shuli! Put a watch on the insider woman's camp."

"Okay."

Crispin poured the last of the lead, holding his breath until the fumes went away. "Got enough melted for a whole clip today."

Pops nodded. "Very good."

Three little boys came in, pushing past his children. "Mr. Hartmann! Mr. Hartmann! We got bullets!"

Crispin laughed. "Let's see them."

Each boy put a destroyed bullet on his desk. "Very good!" He reached into the basket behind him, took out the last three rolls there. "One for each of you."

"Hurray!" The children grabbed the rolls and raced out, whooping with delight.

Crispin tossed the bullets into a bowl. "Come on, Pops, let's go home." He picked up a smaller basket which held a long baguette — he didn't give those out unless a child brought him ten bullets — and put the smaller basket into the bigger one. He handed his father the baskets, picked up his tools, put them in a carrying case, and went outside. Shuli and Wànzi would lock up.

Crispin and Pops turned away from the fence, up the hill towards their home, Crispin's kids trailing along behind.

His grandfather had been put outside the fence for being a drunkard, but had cleaned up after Pops was born. He built a house, and even though Grandpa was dead now, they kept making their home better every year.

Crispin didn't go straight to the house. When he had extra bread like today, Crispin would go past a few places. Old men who had helped his family. The sick. A woman who was newly pregnant, or a family with a lot of small ones. People who could use a little extra. He'd go there at random, break off a good chunk of bread, and give it to them. The gratitude was payment enough, but they always did something for him in return, one way or another.

Once the loaf was gone, he and Pops went home.

The children had run ahead, and his Nana stood at the door waiting for them. "Charlie's here already. Come in and get washed up."

Crispin's younger brother Charlie sat at the table. A huge man with curly red hair — Pops said that came from their mother — he enveloped Crispin in a bear hug. "Guess what? I got the pump mechanism to work. We now got steam-powered automated running water!"

Damn, Charlie's smart. "Shoulda been an Inventor, I'm telling ya!"

Charlie laughed. "Well, maybe I am one. Who needs insider titles, anyways?"

Pops grinned, reaching up to ruffle Charlie's hair. "That's my boy. Come on, let's help Nana with the table."

***

Acevedo sipped his tea in its chipped cup by Katherine's campfire and watched the shadows lengthen, desperately trying one scenario after another in his mind.

Could he invite them to his home? Would that be proper? He didn't have money to put them into a hotel, except perhaps for one night. Who did he know that he could impose upon?

The main thing he knew is that he couldn't stay here overnight; Katherine's reputation would be ruined if he did so. Yet he couldn't leave her in this terrible place.

Finally, he rose. "Come with me."

Katherine and Molly looked at each other. "Where?"

"It doesn't matter. Please, you must come now — once darkness falls, I won't be able to bring you out."

Katherine looked longingly at her little lean-to, then took up a few belongings and hurried alongside him.

No one stood at the gates. Acevedo shouted, "Hey! The sun is still up. Let us out!"

A man ambled by. "The guards went home."

"But that's my conveyance! I came to get these ladies out of here. Now I want you to open this gate immediately!"

The man shrugged. "Don't have the keys, sir. Is there someone I can contact?"

I'll never hear the end of this. "Vincenzo Spadros. 131 West

Shill. The cross-street is Snow. Tell him to hurry."

Molly disappeared behind them at a run, then after several minutes, ran back, distraught. "Ma! They've taken everything — even our dinner!"

Katherine took the weeping girl in her arms.

Acevedo turned to Katherine. "I'm so sorry. I've only made things worse."

What else could I have done?

He patted Molly's shoulder. "There, there, my dear. Don't fret: I'll get you safely out of this place. I promise."

***

It was well into the night before Uncle Vinny arrived. "Sorry it took so long," he said, his breath steaming in the cold air. He glared at the man with the keys. "I had to twist some arms."

"Who is this man?" Katherine said.

Acevedo had given Molly his coat, and his teeth chattered as he spoke. "Mrs. Bluff, may I present my uncle, Vincenzo Spadros."

The huge gate swung open with a squeal.

"A pleasure to meet you, sir," Katherine said.

Acevedo said, "Now let's get you out of this night air."

***

Mama was in a frenzy. "Where have you been? The messenger seemed so agitated! I was distraught with worry —" The instant she saw Katherine, she dropped the Italian, becoming the soul of graciousness. "Oh, my poor dear, come in. I'll make up rooms for you and your daughter. Let me find something for you to wear." She led them away.

Papa padded up in his robe and pajamas. "When you didn't come home I thought something happened. Didn't expect to see two more for breakfast."

"I couldn't let them stay out there," Acevedo said. "It's a freezing junk heap. Ragged children —"

Papa pulled his robe tighter. "I know, son. That Polansky Kerr might not be King yet, but he may as well be. The thugs who drag widows outside the city for not paying his falsely inflated rents are all his, as well as the ones who keep them locked out."

Acevedo knew there were derelicts out there, but **children**? "How did this happen? There were eight-year-olds out there who couldn't remember anything else!"

Papa crossed his arms. "It's that old King Taylor; he's not been outside his palace for decades. As far as I can tell, he spends more effort on gilding the bridges and lining his pockets than figuring out how to make sure everyone's fed."

And the fence has been there since I was a boy.

"Something needs to be done," Acevedo said. "It's the end of September; winter will be here soon. It's not right to leave people in such a state." He paced around, mind reeling. "I can't keep those children from my mind."

What am I to do?

Eventually, his father went to bed. Acevedo sat at the kitchen table with a glass of wine, unable to sleep.

Katherine came out in a robe and sat across the table from him.

Acevedo said, "How's Molly?"

"She's sleeping. It's been a long day for her." She paused, glancing away. "A long year, really."

"Some wine?"

"No, thank you."

An awkwardness lay in the air.

"Sir, I wanted to thank you for your help."

"It was the least I could do. I couldn't let you stay there; it was unsafe for you both."

She smiled to herself. "It's not often you see a teacher so devoted to his students."

"Oh?"

"First you offer Molly a job, then come to rescue her. It's quite touching."

Acevedo felt flustered. "Well — as I said, it would have been wrong to allow the two of you to stay there, when I had the means to help."

Katherine sat gazing at the edge of the table. "When did she die?"

Acevedo blinked. "I beg your pardon?"

"My daughter calls you **Mr.** Spadros. I see no wife here, and you don't look the sort for inappropriate behavior." She paused. "Perhaps I shouldn't have spoken."

The way she said this made him think: *she wants to know what sort of man I am.* Acevedo found that encouraging.

He shook his head. "It was long ago. I was twenty when we married, and we went to Italy for the honeymoon. Six weeks we were gone, and the first night Liza says, 'I have the strangest feeling we've made a child.' I said nothing, but when her blood never came, we saw a doctor in Milan who told us that her feelings were correct. We were so happy."

"What happened?"

"We were back in Bridges, walking through the zeppelin station, when a robbery happened next to us. I never saw it; the police said the man's shot missed its target and hit her."

The memory seemed as vivid as if it happened that day. Her look of surprise as she fell had seared itself in his mind. "She died in my arms."

"I'm so sorry."

"I've been much longer without her than with her." Acevedo pondered that for a while, remembering that golden summer when he was truly happy. "At first I could think of nothing else." He glanced at Katherine. "Someday, the pain you feel now will lessen."

She nodded, eyes downcast, and sat quietly for some time. "Sir, I have no dowry for my daughter. But —"

Acevedo said, "I don't understand."

"You have spoken of my daughter highly. You offered her a job. You came to rescue her, offering her your coat, even bringing her into your home. In six months, she'll be of age. I wanted you to know where we stood, since you've shown your interest so plainly."

He gaped at her "I'm afraid you've misunderstood me, madam. Your daughter is beautiful, intelligent, and hard-working. I'm sure she'll make some young man a fine and dutiful wife. But she's a child, and I'm her teacher. I hold no regard for her in that way." He felt deflated. "I'm sorry."

Katherine appeared taken aback. "My apologies, sir." Their eyes met, and her cheeks reddened. "Oh."

Acevedo said, "I couldn't allow you to remain there." He glanced away, embarrassed. "But don't trouble yourself; think of it as one friend helping another. As soon as you're able, we'll find you a place to stay, should you wish to go."

October 1st

Ocho Malize stood at attention outside the throne room. It was almost the end of his first week in this new post.

Night duty wasn't too bad so far: four hours outside night court, a fifteen minute break, then four hours outside the royal bedchambers. Easy compared to patrolling the halls downstairs. And it was good pay, too. With his wife expecting their first child next spring, the extra money was very welcome.

A group of judges approached, seven old men in robes stopping three paces away. One moved his hand towards his new superior, Arthur Cassino.

Ocho's hand moved to his weapon, but in the judge's hand was a document, which his third took.

"I believe we're expected." The judge glanced at Ocho.

Cassino handed the paper to the judge and nodded.

The clock across the hall chimed the quarter hour. The doors opened by themselves, on a timer.

Cassino had said you could open them whenever you wanted. But this way, they could watch the people coming in and out. Ocho thought it seemed like a good idea.

A group of judges came out. The group outside went in.

"You gotta stop doing that," Cassino said. "Relax. This is about the easiest job you're gonna find. You're not on patrol duty anymore." He turned his face to the setting sun. "Worst thing you'll find here is sore feet."

It seemed to Ocho that security was pretty lax up here, especially with the protests going on all the time. But he wasn't in charge.

A robed figure came down the hall; a woman. Young, pretty. She smiled at Cassino. "Hey Arthur."

"Hey, Tina," Cassino said. "You bring us anything?"

She put her hand in her pocket and came out with a flask. "Can I go see Grandpa? I got a message for him."

"You sure your grandpa won't mind?"

"Oh, no, he's actually expecting it. I'm kind of nervous — I've never been in there this late before."

"Women aren't allowed in night court," Ocho said.

"Shut up, Malize, you're gonna scare the girl." Cassino turned to Tina. "Don't mind him: he's new." He glanced at the clock. "Three minutes til the door opens." Cassino reached out his hand, and she handed him the flask, which he took.

Ocho stared at it, horrified. "What the hell is this? We don't drink on duty."

"Come on, relax. We're here all night." Cassino handed the flask to Ocho across the doorway. "Not gonna hurt you to take a swig."

Ocho hesitated. Did Head Guard Alcatraz know they were out here drinking?

Both of them stared at him. "Goddamnit, Malize," Cassino said. "Hurry up."

Feeling self-conscious, Ocho took the flask, drank the smallest amount he could, and handed it back.

Damn, that's strong stuff.

Cassino took a long drink from the flask, then handed it to Tina. "You're a lifesaver."

She smiled. "Don't mention it."

The doors opened and she went in. The judges didn't come out, but that wasn't unusual; sometimes King Taylor allowed them two slots for important matters.

Ocho didn't dare say anything more. It was clear he had

a lot of adjusting to do. He yawned.

Still got hours to go tonight.

Ocho was starting to wish he hadn't drunk anything. Booze always made him sleepy.

"Don't start that," Cassino said. "You're gonna get me yawning too."

***

Xavier stood next to the King on duty as the night court droned on.

Jack told him an odd story at dinner. A girl — from the way he talked, Xavier thought maybe Jack liked her — had been missing from school for three days. On the third day, Mr. Spadros didn't appear either; the Headmaster taught the class. The girl and Mr. Spadros were both back, several days now. But on his return, Mr. Spadros wished to discuss King Taylor's reign, of all things.

Mr. Spadros had given the students a strange assignment: a report on the history of the fence encircling the city, with extra credit and a prize for the one presenting the most factual account.

*I thought they had just **begun** Bridges history.*

A lot of strange things were happening. His fourth, Alan Whist, found dead in an alley two weeks ago, for one thing. This new man Malize was the best of the downstairs patrol guard, been here for years. But Xavier didn't like to move a man up so quickly. Normally, someone standing so close to the King was vetted and trained for months before starting.

And the police had no clues as to who murdered Whist.

Then a young woman entered, which too was odd: women were normally not allowed in night court.

Why did Cassino let her in?

Xavier exchanged a puzzled glance with his second, Fritz Zepik, who stood on the other side of the King.

The woman was veiled, with fine breasts and a slim waist barely hidden beneath a thin flowing gown, her hips swaying as she passed by them to speak to Polansky Kerr.

Kerr glanced at Xavier and their eyes locked.

It was then Xavier recognized the woman: Tina Kerr, one of the King's great-granddaughters.

The Prince's granddaughter.

Heart pounding, Xavier snapped his focus to the view in front, the judges lined up before them. The woman left several minutes later.

Why was she allowed in? Why did King Taylor not say anything about it?

I shall have to reprimand the Guards outside. His men knew better than this.

The judges left, and when the doors opened once more, Xavier expected the next set of judges. Instead the woman entered, and behind her, several dozen armed men.

Xavier pulled his pistol.

A gurgling sound came to his right. Polansky Kerr stood over King Taylor with a bloody knife, laughing as blood gushed from his father's throat.

Fritz Zepik lay dead, a pool of blood spreading from the gaping wound in his neck.

Is this real? Or is this a nightmare?

"Now, now, Mr. Alcatraz," Polansky Kerr said. "Your second has murdered the King before any of us could stop him. I took my revenge, though, and if you're a smart man, that's what everyone else will hear." His smile grew unpleasant. "If not, I have a man sitting outside your home right now. Jack and Joy. What lovely names. And such lovely children." He wiped his blade, put it away.

Xavier seethed. "You've said what you need to."

"Good." Kerr paused. "Guards!"

No answer.

Terrified, Xavier pushed past Kerr's men, rushed into the hall.

His men lay on the ground. Ocho Malize was unconscious, Arthur Cassino was dead. Xavier knelt beside Arthur's body and screamed, "Guards!"

***

It was almost midnight. Xavier paced outside Malize's hospital room.

Arthur's dead.

What would he tell the man's family? That he suspected the Prince had him killed?

When the doctor emerged, Xavier went to him. "What happened?"

"Poison," the doctor said. "Fortunately, your man here only took in a small amount. He should be improved in the next day or so, but I'd give him a few days before putting him back to work."

"Can I see him?"

The doctor nodded.

Xavier rushed to Malize's side. He had to know who did this. "Ocho, wake up."

Malize moaned.

Xavier patted Malize's cheek. "Wake up."

"Whaa?" Malize opened his eyes.

"Do you remember what happened?"

Malize hesitated, then frowned. "I — the last thing I remember was ... I was at home, getting ready for work." He looked up at Xavier. "What happened?"

"Zepik and Cassino are dead."

Malize stared at Xavier in horror. "Who? How?"

Xavier glanced away.

First Whist, now Cassino and Zepik. Am I next?

What do I do?

"You wouldn't believe it if I told you." Xavier patted Malize's arm. "Just rest, Ocho." He gave Malize as encouraging a smile as he could muster. "Congratulations. You've been promoted. You're my new second, as soon as you're on your feet."

Malize looked as if he were going to be sick.

October 8th

A week after King Taylor's murder, Xavier stood beside Polansky Kerr as the Prince was crowned in front of a cheering crowd.

After his coronation, Polansky Kerr went to the podium. "My beloved people:

"Thank you for your expressions of love and sorrow for my father. He worked tirelessly to help this city prosper. And he was cut down cruelly by a man who cared nothing for his life's work. That man — who hardly deserves that name — was a poor, unwashed boy we in the city of Bridges gave a chance to."

What? Xavier thought. *Fritz was a gentleman, the same as the rest of us.*

"But he took those chances — free education, food and clothing, admission into the Guard, promotion to the Throne Room itself — and spit on it. Just as every person — no, I won't call them people — every FAILURE outside the fence has done. These failures — and many more taking our handouts — are a menace to our way of life. They take and take, yet give nothing in return. They spit on our generosity. They are birthed by loose women, raised into immoral, wanton behavior, grow up on violence, and die having taken your hard work and destroyed it." He shook his fist. "They killed my father. I vow to rid the city of them, if I have to kill every last one."

Xavier and Malize exchanged a horrified glance, then Xavier stared out into the crowd.

This is madness. But he's the King now. What can I do?

October 9th

The classroom was in agitation when Acevedo entered. He shut the door. "Tell me what you're thinking."

Every student raised their hands.

But Molly stood, and the rest of the room quieted. "My mother and I didn't do anything wrong. But men came and took us outside, and I met a lot of good people there. There were some bad, but even they helped us. Mr. Spadros helped us. If it wasn't for him, my Ma and I would be there now. This man wants to kill people like me!" Tears filled her eyes. "There are little children there, old people." She stared at Acevedo with horror. "I think he's not a good King." She sat, putting her head in her hands, weeping as the other girls comforted her.

Jack stood. "My dad's scared. He's in the Throne Guard, and ... I think he saw something the day the King died. He won't talk about it. That's not like him." He shook his head. "Something's wrong."

Something's wrong. The room fell silent.

A chill went down Acevedo's spine. "There's something I want to say."

Everyone stared at him.

"The benevolent monarchy is a good form of government. But monarchy can quickly become —" he almost said malignant, but he didn't want to frighten them,"— can move to dictatorship."

How do I say this so they understand?

"There's a time in the life cycle of every dictatorship where things can be stopped. Where speaking out makes a difference. Past that time, the horror must run its course, and all you can do is flee, fight, or just hide long enough to survive." He took a deep breath, let it out. "I don't know where we are in the cycle. For now, you must say nothing, not to your best friends, your brothers, sisters, not even your parents. I want you all to live through this."

"But what can we **do**?" Jack said.

"For now? Do nothing. I know it's a lot to ask. Sometimes nothing is the most difficult thing to do. You may not be old enough to do it."

That sparked several of them into a renewed courage.

"But you must, if not for your own life, for the lives of your families." Acevedo shook his head. "If you speak out when it's past that point I spoke of, you won't accomplish anything but dying. I must find out what is going on, and whether it can be stopped. And if we can stop this, I assure you, I'll do everything I know of to try."

October 12th

Xavier stood beside King Polansky Kerr, who wore his crown. For what reason, Xavier couldn't tell: this was merely a meeting with his advisors. But since his coronation, Polansky seldom took it off.

A heavy, uncomfortable thing that crown is, King Taylor once told Xavier. *At times I wish I never had to put it on.*

For all his silence in the past, Polansky Kerr seemed to be unable to stop talking now he was King. The glass of Party Time in his hand probably didn't help matters.

King Taylor's former advisors sat nearby, while several scribes took notes of all that was said.

"First we need to clear the streets. Search the parks, the embankments, and under the bridges. Anyone without a home must be moved outside the city. Close down the shelters and move those people outside too. Contact the landlords, the banks — I want the names of anyone who's behind on their bills. They need to go as well."

His adviser sounded astonished. "Is that legal?"

"Who cares? I'm the King. You'll do as I say. Or would you rather go with them?"

The man blanched. "No, sir."

Kerr seemed pleased. "On to the next topic: food. The grain shipments need more guards — we've had two ambushed so far this week."

"Sir," Xavier said.

Kerr turned to him. "What?"

"Permission to speak freely, sir."

"That's 'Your Majesty' to you. Very well. You're the Head of the Guard. What do you have to say?"

"We have no more Guards available to deploy on grain shipments. I've lost four Guardsmen this month already."

"Don't worry about it," Kerr said. "I have men I can use. Bring those others back onto the island."

"Yes, Your Majesty," Xavier said.

"Now, back to the matter at hand. I want all trash trucks dusted with ashes before dumping their loads. We don't need to give those miscreants our hard-earned food. They don't deserve it. And stop those damned women from feeding them!"

"Women?" A scribe said. "What women?"

"Those Dealers."

An advisor said, "How do you suggest we stop them?"

"I don't care. Kill them if you have to."

The men stared at the King in shock. The Dealers were consecrated priestesses for the city's major religion!

Xavier felt stunned. Did he **want** the people to riot?

After a moment's silence, one said, "Yes, your Majesty."

"Once that's done, we'll go through the poor camps and burn them to the ground. Kill them all. Anyone who survives, we hunt down and shoot. Get rid of the freeloaders. Bring Bridges back to its former glory."

"Y-yes, sir. I mean, Your Majesty."

Kerr turned to Xavier. "I want plans drawn up for the attack. Six months from today ought to be enough time to get this ready. March 12th. Make it happen."

Xavier didn't move, didn't breathe. There were over a hundred thousand people past the fence, most of them women and children. What was happening?

October 13th

The next morning as Xavier was preparing to leave, Ocho Malize approached him. "Are we really doing this?"
He's threatened my children. "What do you suggest?"
Malize glanced away. "I don't know."

***

Xavier's children were almost ready for school when Xavier got home. But Jack was unusually quiet at breakfast. "Son, are you well?"
"Dad, we said we would invite Mr. Spadros to dinner."
In all the turmoil, he had forgotten. "I apologize. Ask him if he'll come tonight."
Jack gave a weak smile, and didn't meet Xavier's eye. "Okay, Dad."
After Jack and Joy left for school, Xavier tried to sleep, but couldn't.
Kill them all.
Burn them to the ground.
Anyone who survives, we hunt down and shoot.
This wasn't what he joined the Guard for.
A shocking thought crossed his mind: *I should kill him.*
Xavier was the Head of the Guard, whose primary duty was to the Royal Family. To even think of harming one of them was treason.
Xavier rolled on his side, curled into a ball, head in his

hands, the pressure between his duty and his morals squeezing the life from him.

I can't live like this anymore.

But then he thought: *I can't even kill him in his sleep.*

The Throne Guard had been barred from the royal bed-chambers. In spite of the fact the man was both married and a grandfather, the royal bed-chambers had been turned into Polansky Kerr's playground, with dozens of young women going in and out at all hours. Polansky's men tasted the food, the wine, and supervised the cleaning of plates, which were rewashed before the food was plated. This king was suspicious of everyone.

But what could Xavier do about it? People already looked on **him** with suspicion. Between the King's death and Xavier's sudden demotion — the head of the Guard **always** guarded the royal bed-chambers — rumors were flying that he had been negligent somehow.

He remembered the woman in the room. *She was a trap,* he thought, ashamed and angry. *She certainly trapped **me**.*

And now the King was dead.

***

Helena Deschapelles, Director of the Dealers and Keeper of the Cathedral, looked up from her desk in surprise. "Are you certain?"

Her assistant Octavia Underlead handed over the report. "Read it for yourself."

> Surveillance report: direct order to the Office of the Police Commissioner from the Office of the King — prevent Dealers from offering aid to constituents outside the Pot of Gold, such order to be enforced by all means necessary including death. Effective immediately. Noted by my hearing and sight this 13th

of October.

Pianola Seed, Dealers Intelligence.

Helena stood. "Call a meeting at once."

She paced her office. This was the tenth in a series of reports coming in from all over the city. Trash being sprayed with ashes. The elderly taken from their homes without warning, then dumped outside the fence. Gentlemen beaten and dragged outside the city after falling asleep on a park bench.

Something was happening, and it wasn't good.

For three hundred years the Dealers had protected the city of Bridges on direct orders from the Kings, beginning with the Inventor King himself. But unlike the others, on taking the throne this King hadn't sought their report: instead, he had turned against them.

King Taylor didn't trust his son.

He must have meant to give the secret knowledge of the Heart of Bridges to another.

King Taylor was an old man; perhaps he had already done so. One of the grandsons, perhaps?

Moving to her cabinet, she pulled out the long drawer of files on Polansky Kerr. Evidence supported the suspicion that Taylor Kerr's death wasn't an assassination by his guard, as his son asserted, but patricide.

Octavia returned. "We await you, Director."

Around the oval table sat her most trusted advisers. Helena gazed at the white marble walls, the stained glass windows depicting the Acts of the Dealer throughout the ages, the symbols of the Holy Cards surrounding them.

Blessed Dealer, guide me, she prayed. Thousands of women's lives depended on her decision today.

"My beloved sisters, it is clear we have a threat to the Dealers' future, and by extension, to Bridges itself. But this is the tournament the Dealer has presented to us, the reason our hands have been dealt onto the Grand Board at this time and not another. We must take the long view, not base all our actions on one play of the cards. The Dealers must never fail our people. So I have come to a decision: we must cease handouts at once."

Murmurs filled the room.

"However, this does not mean we give up aid. Rather, we increase it. We build more places for the people to go. Aid stations will now be engaged with providing the elderly, the pregnant, and widows work in exchange for food and bed. We shall become an employer." She smiled. "Surely Polansky Kerr, of all people, would want to see his citizens busy."

Scattered laughter.

"Everything shall be documented, and if the police wish to close us down, that will be documented as well. We shall offer no resistance in word or gaze; we will simply slip into the crowd, send our evidence to safety, then return when they leave."

"A scissors play," one woman said.

"Exactly," said Helena. "We deliberately lose. But only for this round. My sisters, this city is no longer ruled by men, but by boys. And boys love to win. We will let them win and win and win until they choke on it. Until they destroy themselves."

And at the end, we shall hold the high cards.

Octavia raised her hand. "Director, is this the only way?"

She's afraid.

Helena nodded. "We are unarmed." She raised her hand to forestall the inevitable objection. "If it comes to that, and we reveal that card and fail, at best, the city is hostage. At worst, Bridges is lost. I will not betray everything we swore to uphold to forestall our deaths for a few moments against a mob which we can never defeat without aid." She spoke gently. "It would be the coward's way out."

Octavia flushed, her head down, but she nodded.

Helena gazed at the image of the Blessed Dealer, for a moment wondering what history would make of all this.

This could be my last decision as Director. But hopefully

someone will survive to remember.

Helena shook her head. "If it does come to that, we must appear to have been defeated here. They may win, yet the Dealers — and Bridges — will survive."

***

Acevedo looked up from his desk after class: Jack Alcatraz stood there. "Mr. Spadros, may I speak with you?"

"Certainly. Sit, please."

Since his declaration the other day, Jack had become more and more withdrawn. Acevedo suspected his father's problem — whatever it was — gave Jack cause to worry. Today, the boy seemed tired.

"We'd like to have you for dinner tonight."

Acevedo smiled. "I'd enjoy that, thank you."

"Would you speak with my dad?"

"About what?"

Jack glanced away. "Something happened yesterday, something bad. I don't know ... I can feel it, my dad's ..."

"Bothered by it?"

"Yeah." Jack shook his head, just a bit. "He won't talk to me. I know I'm just a kid. I get it. He doesn't want me to worry. But ..."

Acevedo smiled. "He needs a friend."

"Yeah. That's it." Jack relaxed.

Acevedo reached over, patted the boy's shoulder. "You've done well. I'll be glad to talk to him."

"Thanks, Mr. Spadros."

Acevedo felt touched by the boy's trust in him. Since the talk with the class, Acevedo hadn't learned much of anything. But he had begun to call on his former students, just to see how they felt and what they knew, and to ask about their classmates. He told them he planned a reunion, and each was pleased to tell him more.

He pulled out a chart. So far, he had over 100 names of those who he had either contacted (just a few) or who personally knew others that still lived in Bridges. Acevedo set a special mark on the ones who were labeled "trouble" —

those might be the very ones who could help, if it came down to violence.

Acevedo wasn't sure what he was going to do with this chart, but he might need help, and these were the people most likely to help him.

Rolling up the chart, he took it with him. This was something he didn't want anyone else seeing.

***

Xavier put the dishes in the sink to soak, and turned to Mr. Spadros. "Some wine?"

"Yes, thank you."

Jack and Joy had left the table early, which was odd: Xavier expected Jack would want to spend time with his teacher. Xavier set the wine bottle and glasses on the table, and began to pour. "Jack said you were ill recently. I hope you're improved?"

Mr. Spadros nodded. "Very much so."

Xavier didn't know who else to turn to. But he hesitated. *Should I put this man in danger?*

"I wanted to thank you for reassuring your students."

"Oh?"

"Jack told me his classmates were upset by recent events, but that you spoke to them and now they feel much encouraged."

Mr. Spadros gave the slightest of smiles. "I'm glad I could be of help."

The man almost seemed as if he were waiting for something. "What do you think of the recent events?"

Now Mr. Spadros hesitated. "I understand why they might feel upset by them."

Xavier had a sudden insight: *This man is a teacher of history. Today, we're in history.* "Two forty-seven."

Mr. Spadros smiled. "So you remember your coursework, after all these years."

In the year 247 After the Catastrophe, a warlord assassinated the leader of the United American Survivors. After eight years of genocide against the Krissins, he and his men were overthrown by a collaboration between rebel forces and a traitor in his own ranks.

He understands the situation, Xavier thought. *He's here to help.* "Let's take a walk."

Surprise crossed his former teacher's face, but Mr. Spadros rose, put on his coat and Derby hat, and followed Xavier out to the street.

Xavier turned right and went past the row of homes, towards the shops, speaking softly. "There's a possibility we're being watched."

"Oh?"

"My children's lives were threatened."

"Oh."

"By Polansky Kerr." Xavier refused to call that madman a king.

Mr. Spadros didn't speak for some time. "Jack told me something happened. Was that it?"

Xavier was so disoriented by the question that he stopped in his tracks.

How has it come to this?

He faced Mr. Spadros. "This was after he killed my second, a man I've known for over twenty years, then murdered King Taylor." For a moment, he couldn't speak as the images flooded his mind. "Cut their throats right in front of me, so fast I couldn't stop it." He had to make his teacher understand. "I couldn't stop it!"

Mr. Spadros held on Xavier's upper arms. "Xavier. Look at me. Breathe."

"Is he well?" A woman stood a few paces away, peering at Xavier with concern.

"He just got bad news," Mr. Spadros said. "Come on, son, I'll take you home."

The woman smiled and nodded, then went off.

She thinks he's my father.

Now that he considered it, that was how Xavier felt. He and his actual father never spoke much, unless the old man wanted something.

They walked along, Mr. Spadros grasping Xavier by the upper arm with one hand, his other behind Xavier's upper back. Xavier stopped. "There's more. He means to kill them all. The outsiders. The people, outside the fence. Burn their homes to the ground, then hunt the survivors like animals."

Mr. Spadros turned pale. "Are you certain?"

Xavier spoke in a whisper. "For gods' sake, I stood next to him as he planned it!"

After a moment, Mr. Spadros said, "We'll have to do our best not to let that happen."

Xavier felt a surge of relief. If anyone could find a way out of this, it would be Mr. Spadros.

Mr. Spadros said, "When will it happen?"

"March 12th."

When they returned home, a sudden fear struck: *my children are asleep, alone, defenseless. And Polansky Kerr has threatened them.*

Xavier rushed to his children's rooms.

Even though they both slept peacefully, for the first time in his life, he didn't feel safe in his own home. His hands shook. "I can't stay here anymore," he whispered.

Mr. Spadros, standing behind him, kept his voice low. "You'll have to. If we do anything different, the men who watch will report it to the King. The best way to keep them safe is to make him believe you're on his side."

On his side?

They walked to the front room.

"I'll send a note with Jack," Mr. Spadros said in a normal tone. "Some extra credit assignments, and thoughts as to how you might help him with his studies."

Xavier nodded. *He thinks someone listens even now.* "I appreciate you coming by."

Mr. Spadros clapped him on the shoulder. "My pleasure, sir. Thanks for dinner, it was excellent."

Xavier couldn't remember what they had eaten until he closed the door and faced the dishes in the sink. But it didn't matter. For the first time in a while, he had hope.

***

As Acevedo got into his steam automobile and returned home, a glance behind him made him appreciate his Uncle Vinny for the first time. They used to play Who's Following with his brothers growing up, and these men were amateurs.

Papa always said: *Family is everything*. Acevedo just felt as if he had gained a whole new one. Xavier Alcatraz might be a Throne Guard, but he was badly out of his depth here.

I'm not too close behind, Acevedo thought. He could only imagine what his Uncle Vinny would say when he heard about this.

***

"A history teacher trying to take on the whole city. Well, it could be worse," Uncle Vinny said.

Acevedo laughed in spite of himself. "How?"

Uncle Vinny grinned and clapped a hand to Acevedo's shoulder. "You might not have me helping you."

The thought of his uncle helping him didn't exactly make Acevedo feel any better.

"Look," Uncle Vinny said. "I know you're good at history, and military strategy, and all that book shit. But this is gonna be war. Real war. In the dirt gang carnage. We're gonna have to do things you won't like. Deal with people you wouldn't trust to slop pigs. Bad things will happen."

Acevedo nodded. He knew that, in a theoretical sense. But ... "I just want to keep those children from getting hurt."

"Dammit, Acevedo, you're not listening. Most of those children will die. If not from the war, from the aftermath — the food supply disruptions, the bandits, hell, just the shock of it all. Their parents will die. A lot of those who fight will die. Everyone will lose what they have now. They may end up cursing your name on both sides. Do you understand?"

Uncle Vinny peered at him. "Do you want to get rid of Polansky Kerr or not?"

Yes, Acevedo thought. "They're going to die for sure if we don't do anything."

"Just remember that when you start wondering if it was worth it."

49

October 17th

It was Saturday, and the weather was nice for October, sunny and warm. Xavier sat on his front porch, holding the letter from Mr. Spadros in hand.

Mr. Alcatraz:

If Jack does these extra credit assignments, I'm sure he'll succeed. I even have some prizes for him, should he do well.

1) A report on the Armory — a red firework. I know how much he loves them. It's imperative he do this assignment first.

2) A report on the Royal Family — a blue firework. I'm looking forward to his accomplishing this assignment. He must turn it in by the end of class at 3:00.

If these are completed on the date we discussed, nothing further will be needed. If these assignments are not completed in a timely manner, we'll need to bring the situation outside the classroom.

I have every confidence in your ability to help create the success we both desire. If you have any questions please feel free to contact me.

My Most Sincere Regards,

Acevedo Spadros

Xavier understood the why. He knew what needed to be done: seize the Armory, capture the Royal Family. He even knew why they must secure the Armory first: they had to control the weapons.

Doing it the other way round could fail if Polansky Kerr's supporters had the presence of mind to arm themselves. The Guard could find themselves under siege — and if his supporters were anything like the King, the lives of the Royal Family would mean nothing to them. They'd storm the palace, and it'd be all over.

But he couldn't get away from this fact: *Mr. Spadros wants **me** to be the traitor.*

Xavier had respected and admired his teacher since he first met the man. But Xavier was Head of the Guard. Could he go against his vows? Commit treason?

Xavier listened to the birds chirp, the children play under the apple trees lining the street.

The plan Mr. Spadros gave him was good, but it was by no means guaranteed: bloodless military coups were rare. If he failed to capture Polansky Kerr, the rest of this letter meant civil war, unleashing its most violent members on the city. All this would be gone.

I have to choose which half of the city to save.

He leaned back, disheartened. It was more complicated than that. Polansky Kerr lusted for control, for domination. When he had killed all the poor in Bridges, he'd find some new group to blame and kill. And on, and on, until he either died or was brought down.

In 247, was there a man who could have stopped that horror but didn't?

Xavier didn't want to be that man.

There were well over five months before the attack. Perhaps he could contact the Feds — surely they'd be interested in stopping genocide.

No, Xavier thought. If Polansky Kerr got one inkling of it, Jack and Joy would be dead. And from what he remembered of history, the Feds were just as likely to seal the Aperture (the only way in or out of this dome), let the matter run its course, then seize the city. Hundreds of thousands might be dead by then, the survivors exiled to other cities for the remainder of their lives.

Xavier spread out the crumpled letter in his hands as the Riverfront Train's whistle blew off to his left in the distance.

Seize the Armory, capture the King.

That's all he had to do, by three am on March the 12th, and they'd be free.

I can do this.

He was a guard, not a soldier. But he could learn, and he could train his men. This didn't have to be a civil war. Both sides of the fence were worth saving, and if he could save the entire city, Xavier decided, he would.

***

Blocker Goolsby went past. He could tell when a man wasn't in a mood to talk, and Mr. Alcatraz hadn't been in a talking mood the last few times he'd been by. His children seemed well — it was strange. But then he remembered that the man was in the palace guard.

I guess I wouldn't feel like talking much either, having to be around that hateful old King all day.

"Hey, Blocker," Mr. Alcatraz called out.

"Hey, Mr. Alcatraz." He didn't go to the porch. *I'll wait to see if he wants me over there.*

"Listen, I got a question for you."

Blocker went to the porch, just past the steps, and leaned his hand on the support. "Whatcha need?"

"You know anyone who's —" Mr. Alcatraz hesitated. "For example, if you thought someone was going to break into your house, hurt your family."

Damn, Blocker thought. *No wonder he's not in a talking mood these days.* "I know someone who can help you. You want them gone, or you want protection?"

Mr. Alcatraz gave Blocker a smile.

He knows who's after him. He's going after the guy himself.

"Protection. For my children."

Cold rage. "You leave that to me. No charge."

Mr. Alcatraz seemed surprised. "You sure?"

"Damn straight. You live in Wheelcard territory, Mr. Alcatraz. No one's gonna come here and fuck with anyone in **our** area, 'specially not a Guardsman's children."

The relief on the man's face made Blocker feel like he was doing something worthwhile. Blocker reached out his hand. "Don't worry about a thing, Mr. Alcatraz — we'll take good care of you."

***

Like Xavier, Acevedo and Uncle Vinny sat on the front porch, but they were drinking beer.

"So what's your plan?" Vinny said. "How do you want to get this started?"

"Well," Acevedo said, "we should find out who in the city is against the King. I'll begin with my former students. Just simple questions: What do you think of the new King? How do you think he's doing so far? If the person seems amenable, I'll say I want to do something about this. Who do you trust the most that might be willing to help?"

"Wrong," Uncle Vinny said. "Completely wrong. The people in this city don't care. If they did, the fence wouldn't be up in the first place. They're not going to risk destroying their homes and livelihoods for a bunch of poor people."

Acevedo felt deflated. "What do you suggest then?"

"We gotta get to the people who do care. The ones outside the fence."

"Okay."

"And we gotta get muscle." He shifted in his chair. "That's gonna be the hard part."

"Muscle?" When Acevedo had written to Xavier, he had only a vague notion of who might be fighting — more a populist "storm the Bastille with pitchforks" scenario than anything else. This sounded like his uncle had something more plausible.

"You know," Vinny said. "The gangs. The Families. The clans." He paused. "But we got your back, Ace. Your Papa agreed: the Spadros Family's in, all the way."

Acevedo stared at his uncle in shocked disbelief.

His uncle smirked. "You really don't know."

"Know what, Uncle Vinny?"

Spadros was a common name in Bridges: the Spadros brothers were architects from Chicago who helped Benjamin Kerr design the city. Acevedo always thought that the Spadros crime family was just a group with their same name. "The Spadros Family — it's us?"

"Acevedo, you may be a smart guy, but you're a dumb guy, you know what I mean? Where did you think your father got the money to send you to school, to raise ten children, send you and Liza to Italy, buy you that fancy steam automobile, let you play with maps and toys all your life? Huh?"

Acevedo never considered the matter.

"Have you ever seen him go off to work?"

Acevedo thought back. "Well, no. But I just thought —"

Uncle Vinny laughed. "That Trapasso Spadros was a gentleman of independent means? Wait till I tell him that!" He shook his head, amused. "Listen, kid, we get things done around here. Someone here got a problem, they come to me, and I send guys to fix it. If it means busting a few heads, I send someone to do that too. Used to do it myself, but I'm getting too old for that now. I have one of your little brothers do it, or one of your cousins."

Acevedo couldn't believe what he was hearing. Papa was a criminal? His brothers were beating up people?

"Why didn't Papa tell me?"

Uncle Vinny shrugged. "You just weren't the sort. Plus, you're good for our cover. You're an educated man. A highly respected teacher in a private high school." He pulled at his collar with both hands, grinning. "You give us class."

Acevedo felt bitter. "So all these years you've despised me, huh?"

"Nah, not at all. You do your part, the same as everyone else." He clapped Acevedo on the shoulder. "We love you, scamp. You're family. No one despises you."

Acevedo set his beer down on the floor between his feet, put his head in his hands. He felt as if the ground had fallen out from underneath him.

Everything he thought was true was a lie.

Uncle Vinny got up, taking his beer with him. "You feel like talking again, you let me know."

Acevedo heard the front screen open and shut. He raised his head and looked around. **Really** looked around.

Children played, women chatted on porches, men sat in front of shops way down the street drinking espresso. Clocks sat atop fancy lamp posts which were lit every evening. But men just a bit overdressed wearing dark spectacles stood on corners in twos and threes, smoking, chatting, watching everything.

Acevedo had seen them all his life, never thought anything of it before. Those men came over all the time. His family went to their homes for dinner. They played ball with him when he was little.

But they were mobsters. It seemed incomprehensible. *How did I not see it?*

October 18th

Xavier peeked outside.

Blocker stood there next to a big guy with thinning brown hair.

This felt strange; Blocker had never rung the doorbell before. Xavier opened the door.

"Hey, Mr. Alcatraz," Blocker said, "this is the guy I was talking about."

The man stuck out a hand. "Call me Turbo."

Xavier shook the man's hand. "Good to meet you."

Xavier wasn't sure what the protocol was for this sort of thing. "Would you like to come in?"

"Won't be necessary," Turbo said. "Just wanted to meet the kids."

Xavier nodded. "Jack! Joy!"

They came running down the stairs.

"This is Mr. Turbo —"

"Just Turbo is fine."

"Anyway, you might see him around. He'll help you. You know Blocker, right?"

The kids seemed shy. "Yeah, we know him," Jack said.

"Well, if anything happens, you can trust them. Like if something happens when I'm not here." Xavier felt flustered. "I'm going to have to be at work a lot for a while."

"Okay, Dad," Jack said. "Nice to meet you, Turbo." They

retreated, whispering between themselves.

Xavier felt relieved. Maybe this Blocker was more useful than he thought.

The best way to keep your children safe is to make Kerr believe you're on his side. "Do you know anyone that's been to war?"

The men seemed confused.

"You know, military?"

They shook their heads.

Wait, my dad was in the Army, Xavier thought.

As much as Xavier hated going to him, that might be the best way to get what he was looking for.

"Well, I'll let you get back to your family," Turbo said.

"I appreciate you coming by," Xavier said. "I feel a lot better knowing someone else is looking out for them."

When Xavier closed the door, Jack said, "That guy looks like a thug."

"Probably is," Xavier said, "but I need help, and he's who we have. You can trust him."

"Why do we need help, Dad?" Joy said. "Is someone after us? What's going on?"

"Don't worry about it." Xavier hugged both of them at once. "You're safe; that's all that matters." He let go of them. "Want to go see Grandpa?"

His children looked at him as if he had gone insane.

***

His father opened the door. "Xavier? Never thought I'd see you here!"

"Hi, Grandpa," Jack said.

Joy hung back.

How long has it been?

"You remember Joy, don't you, Dad?"

His father grinned. "When I last saw you, you were a little girl. Now look at you!" He hugged the children in turn. "How old are you now, sixteen?"

"Next summer," Joy said. She looked pleased that he missed high instead of low.

"Well, come on in!" From the smell of it, he'd already

begun drinking. "What can I do for you? You want anything to drink?"

"Sure, Dad."

"I got hot tea, lemonade, beer, and whiskey."

Jack got tea, Joy lemonade, and Xavier got a beer. His father filled a tall iced tea glass with whiskey and they sat around the kitchen table. "So what's going on?"

"I was wondering if you have any books or anything from when you were in the Army."

"What kind of books?"

Xavier wasn't exactly sure what he wanted was called. "Urban battle tactics?"

His father gaped at him, then quickly recovered. "Lemme go see." He turned back. "You kids like photographs? I got a whole book of them from when your Daddy was little."

Jack and Joy glanced at each other. Jack said, "Sure." The two of them got up and followed their grandfather into the other room.

Xavier listened to his father locate the photo albums, explain each one, and set them on a table. After a few minutes, he came back with a stack of books. "This is what I have. Not sure why you need them or what you're gonna do with them, but they're yours."

"I just need them for the weekend, Dad."

"Well, I don't need them anymore. Could use the room. So here." He shoved them into Xavier's hands. "Do what you want with them."

"I appreciate it." Xavier set them down beside his beer.

His father glanced back, then put his arms on the table and spoke in a whisper. "Son, what's going on?"

"What do you mean?"

"I haven't seen you in ten years, then you show up at my door asking for war manuals, of all things. What's that madman planning now?"

It was Xavier's turn to gape at his father.

"I can't talk about it," he said. Then he thought: *If this goes wrong, he might be in danger too.* "Have you ever considered moving to the countryside?"

His father nodded, as if he thought he figured out what was going on. "Just say the word. Can't stand this place since your mother died anyway." He paused. "Might be best for me to leave the city altogether."

He grabbed his glass with both hands, knuckles white. "Hate to leave you here, son. But if what's gonna happen is what I think is gonna happen, I'm not going to be much use to you anyway."

October 19th

Xavier stood next to Polansky Kerr, same as always. But when night court was complete, Xavier said, "Permission to speak, Your Majesty."

His second, Ocho Malize, gave him a startled glance.

Polansky Kerr turned, curiosity on his face. "Yes?"

"It occurred to me that if you intend to deploy the Guard to complete the mission outside the fence, then they will require additional training."

"Oh?"

"The Guard has not been trained to take action in close quarters against unarmed civilians."

"I see. What might happen if this training doesn't occur?"

"Casualties, refusal to fight, and desertion are three possible outcomes, Your Majesty. I've set up an extensive small-group training regimen which I'd like to present for your approval."

"Just tell them if they don't fight, I'll kill their families."

Malize, standing behind the King, went pale.

Xavier forced his face to remain still. "That is an additional layer of security you may add if you wish, Your Majesty. However, proper training will enable them to do their jobs in an efficient manner — with or without the threat of violence."

Polansky Kerr nodded. "I see that you've given this

some thought."

"I'm Head of the Bridges Guard, Your Majesty. My job is to ensure the most efficient use of Guard resources while ensuring the safety of the King and his family."

Xavier stared straight ahead, but he could see the gears turn from the corner of his eye as Polansky Kerr peered at him. "Very well. Go ahead. I don't care what you do; just have the men ready when I need them. Understand?"

"Yes, Your Majesty."

Polansky's face became shrewd. "I've changed my mind. Put it on my desk. Let me look it over."

"Of course, Your Majesty. I'll have it on your desk within the hour."

"Very good. Dismissed."

Xavier went to his office, retrieved a thick folder, and placed it on Kerr's desk. Xavier had spent half the night designing the regimen, which he didn't plan to use at all. His true regimen would look enough like this to fool a casual observer without any military training.

This wasn't over yet. Polansky Kerr didn't trust him; this "change of mind" was designed to throw him off balance, discover any discrepancies, any hints of his true plan.

One step at a time, he thought. Even if the man came to half-trust him, it would be enough.

October 20th

With Vinny's help, Acevedo began the slow process of contacting the numerous gangs, crime families, and "clubs" throughout the city.

Acevedo wanted to meet with the smartest ones. "The ones who'll see the value of what we're doing, and what we're up against. Right hand men, the powers behind the leader. You know, men who make the decisions."

Uncle Vinny nodded. "I got a place you can meet up. It's off a dirt road maybe ten miles in the countryside. A scientific station where they tend the city generator, but the building itself's not used much anymore. They give tours once in a while, but most of the workers do their science stuff underground. They didn't seem to mind when I met some guys there last time."

"Sounds good," Acevedo said. "Make sure they know we're coming. I don't want some Inventor's Apprentice high on Party Time shooting at me."

His uncle laughed. "Sure thing, scamp. Anything else?"

An idea was beginning to form. *I can bring the children there during the battle. They should be safe enough. And they wanted to know about the Generator.* "What about weapons?"

"Well, we got plenty of small stuff already, and rocket launchers. We're gonna need ray cannon to breach the fences, though."

Acevedo nodded. "Get some then."

Something kept nagging at him. *Maybe a new set of eyes will help.* "What's to keep the Kerrs from reinforcing?"

"What do you mean, reinforcing?"

"Come here," Acevedo said, and brought his uncle into his room. A map of Bridges lay on the table, the fence marked out in black. "Even if Xavier Alcatraz can capture the island and has enough men to hold the bridges, what's to stop the Kerrs from moving all their men to one bridge and forcing their way through?"

Uncle Vinny peered at the map for a moment, lips pursed. "You gotta blow the bridges."

Acevedo stared at his uncle in horror. "All of them?"

"No, dummy — these ones right here." He pointed to the bridges connecting the downtown quadrants to each other. "You're gonna want to get to the island, right? But what you don't want is for them to get to each other. Blow all four at once. Boom." He peered at Acevedo. "It's the only way, scamp. You gotta do it before you do anything else."

Acevedo pictured those magnificent golden bridges, broken at the bottom of the river. Was this worth it?

If Xavier captured Polansky Kerr, he'd signal with the blue firework, and destroying them wouldn't be necessary.

But his uncle was right: they couldn't take any chances. "That's going to take a lot of explosives."

"I'll get on it."

"Uncle Vinny, where are we getting the money for this?"

"Don't worry, your Papa said you get all the cash you need." He smiled. "He's very proud of you."

For some reason, this made Acevedo happier than it reasonably should. *Papa's head of a crime family. I should hate and despise him.*

But when I needed him, he was there.

"I'm sorry for the disrespect I've given you over the years. You've been good to me."

"Don't worry about it," Vinny said, but Acevedo could tell he was secretly pleased. "Family is everything."

***

After speaking with the King the night before, Xavier had written a requisition for a new training building.

He also had left a note for his assistant, Peter Moysian, to split the men up into groups of twenty, scheduling them to attend half-hour meetings.

When Xavier entered the room for the first meeting, the men sat attentively. Such meetings like this had been rare up to now. "We have a new assignment which is going to require extra training. On March 12, we travel to the fence and set the poor camps on fire."

Polansky Kerr had said nothing about secrecy. Xavier hoped the men would tell others about the plan; a public outcry might dissuade Kerr from going through with it.

Xavier's men glanced at each other, appalled.

"If any survive, we go out in squads and shoot them. No survivors are to remain." He watched as the news sank in.

A man raised his hand. "Are you **sure** this is the order?"

"Yes, Guardsman, directly from the King's mouth as he spoke it to me."

Another man said, "Even the women and children?"

"Yes." Xavier stood quietly as the shock and horror in the room turned to angry muttering. "I have set time for each of you to speak with me personally about our orders, so I may answer any questions you have. Please have your questions ready when Guardsman Malize calls your name."

Xavier sat behind the desk, the room buzzing with conversation. A chair sat next to the end of one side of the desk; Ocho Malize stood at the other end.

Xavier had his assistant schedule his groups — and the order he spoke to the men — by their psychological profiles. The most volatile he put first, as they were the most likely to do something like try to kill the King themselves if they heard about this from someone else. He didn't need any more dead men.

"Quint Varkonyi," Malize said.

A thin, nervous man got up, came over, and sat in the

chair beside him.

"Mr. Varkonyi, do you have thoughts, comments, or questions about this mission?"

"You're damn right I do. I quit."

"I understand your feelings completely."

Varkonyi stared at him. "You do?"

"I have room on the roster for a different mission. Would you be interested?"

"Depends on what the mission was."

"I must tell you that this mission is secret. I can't let you know the details unless you swear yourself to silence."

"Can I resign if I don't want that one either?"

"Of course. As long as you don't betray the Guard."

"What kind of man do you think I am?"

Xavier said, "A brave and honorable one." He took a deep breath and spoke quietly. "This is very important. You must promise not to react."

Varkonyi nodded.

"Most of these men around you are angry. But some like this kind of thing. If you're too happy, they'll know something's up."

Varkonyi said, "You think we got spies?'

"Quint, I don't know anything. But you must promise to act normal."

"Right."

"I plan to remove this King."

Varkonyi stared at him for a long moment. "Damn!" He hit the desk with his fist. Every man in the room turned towards them. He leaned over and whispered, "I got your back, sir. Whatever you need."

"Thank you, Varkonyi. Dismissed."

Malize stared at him, mouth open.

Xavier said casually, "Call the next man, Ocho."

"Uh, yes, sir."

They went through all twenty men in turn. After the last man left, Malize said, "You're really gonna do it. Take down the King."

Xavier said, "Assuming we don't all get killed first."

***

By the end of the week, Xavier had met with each of his small groups, explaining the mission to them as it was presented to him by the King. To each one who seemed uncomfortable, Xavier offered the new mission. Ninety-nine per-cent took it.

***

It turned out Xavier got to use his fake regimen after all. Once the remaining men saw they would be ordered to fire on pregnant women and crying children, several of them turned in their resignations. He offered them the new mission a second time, and the relief on their faces gave him a great deal of encouragement.

Two weeks later, Xavier told the five that were left that they were part of a top-ranked squad that wouldn't be training with the others anymore.

He assigned Ocho Malize to train these men. "I need help so I can get the others ready. Can you do this?"

The man read over the regimen, then grimaced, not meeting Xavier's eye.

Xavier grinned. "Don't worry. Just keep them busy. I may have use for them later."

November 8th

The scientific building Uncle Vinny picked out for the meeting with the crime faction leaders was a utilitarian pale greenish-gray that reminded Acevedo of a hospital. The white-robed Apprentices at the courtyard gates didn't give their group a second glance as they passed by.

It was an odd building, two stories and U-shaped. Torches stood around a large courtyard, which was mostly lined with boxes and old machinery. The ground was grassy and dry.

Acevedo's younger brothers had set up chairs, then retreated to scout for anyone watching.

The group, over a hundred of the roughest men Acevedo had ever seen, nevertheless had intelligent eyes, full of cunning.

Uncle Vinny locked the courtyard gates, then Acevedo stood in front of them. "I'm Acevedo Spadros. How would you like to take over the city?"

The men stared at each other in amazement.

"Polansky Kerr is mad," Acevedo said, his breath steaming in the frosty air. "He murdered King Taylor and plans to kill everyone outside the fence with fire and lead. Even the children."

Angry murmurs came from the men.

"But we plan a surprise for him. I need your help, and

the support of your men. In exchange, you'll get —" He hesitated. *I didn't think this through.* "Whatever you can get."

"Looting rights," Uncle Vinny said from the back.

It sounded much worse when said that way. But he needed these men desperately, and if a few looted homes was what it took, that seemed a small price to pay.

A man with very dark skin stood up. "So we help you get rid of this mad King, and we get to take what we want. No prosecution?"

"Do we look like fucking cops?" Uncle Vinny said.

"Nah, but once this is done, I don't wanna rope round my neck," another man said. "I know you, but I don't know this guy." He faced Acevedo. "Are we here to do your dirty work then get strung up for it?"

The crowd murmured.

"None of that," said Acevedo. "There will be no ropes, so long as you stop when we say. After, we'll need the people behind us, or we'll **all** hang."

Nods scattered around the room.

A short, wiry man with white-blond hair stood. "If Vinny vouches for this guy, that's good enough for me. What's the plan?"

Acevedo had made up large boards with the city mapped out. "There will be two fireworks above Market Center: one red, one blue. Blue means the King was captured and they don't need us. If we don't see the blue one by 3 am, we're blowing the bridges between the quadrants. That'll be the signal." Four bridges blowing at once would be heard halfway to the Rim.

"We'll have ray cannon to breach the fence. Bring all the weapons and ammo you can; we have more for those without. Rocket launchers, the works." He paused. "Don't cross the bridges onto the island. We have people there to secure it and I don't want them shooting you by mistake. They'll wear white armbands to identify themselves."

"Damn," a huge red-haired man said. "You're serious."

"Dead serious," said Uncle Vinny. "If one word gets to

him first, he'll kill us all. So no sneaks, no leaks. Got it?"

That seemed to sober many of them, and they sat, hand to chin, pondering their situation.

Acevedo looked around. "Who's in?"

The blond wiry man laughed. "I figured we had no choice once we saw your faces."

Acevedo shrugged. Forcing people to fight never worked. They had to want it. "Who loves this King?" Silence. "Who loves loot?"

A cheer rang out.

"Not sure why anyone wouldn't do this," the big red-haired man said. "What's the catch?"

Acevedo laughed. "If we fail, I sure hope you can run, because Polansky Kerr will never stop chasing us."

***

Blocker peered at the men around him in the courtyard. He'd fought many of them in the past, and they nodded to each other warily. Vinny had told them: *This is neutral territory, safe passage night,* but Blocker still felt twitchy about getting home.

It didn't take an Inventor to figure out who the people "securing" Market Center would be. *No wonder Mr. Alcatraz is jumpy. He's right in the middle of it. I better warn Turbo that Polansky Kerr's men might be sniffing around.*

But what a plan! Everyone working together to take down Polansky Kerr.

He climbed on his horse and galloped into town. Just wait until he told his brother Fish about this.

***

"So let me get this straight," Fish said. "Kerr kills the King, blames it on a guard, and now he's gonna kill all the outsiders. So why do **we** care?"

"Dammit, we gotta care," Blocker said. "We don't got much territory out there. But we got a lot in here, and if damn near a hundred gangs are gonna get free looting, sooner or later some of them are gonna look at us. We gotta be ready."

His brother's eyes widened. "So what do we do?"

That was a good question. "We gotta pick," Blocker said. "Do we stay in, or try to grab land out there?"

Either was risky. But there were no buildings to speak of outside the fence. "I say make like we're in this, but when it starts, we pull everyone in. There's nothing worth taking out there. Let go of the outside stuff and make damn sure no one takes what's here. They'll get tired of fighting us, move on to easy prey. Once that's done, they'll start fighting each other. While they're doing that, we can start expanding. Introduce ourselves, help the people rebuild, make sure they know we can protect them better than their gang did." Blocker considered the areas around their territory. "We could double our turf if we play our cards right."

Fish nodded. "Let's do it."

***

After the meeting broke up, Acevedo toured the science building. It had two stories: the upper level seemed to mostly be storage. The lower level was set up like a museum. There were displays under glass of the history of the founding of the city. Descriptions of how it was powered by the Magma Steam Generators below the pilings which anchored the vast dome mechanism of the city to the bedrock. Details of how the rivers were filtered.

There were several rooms full of displays covering the different topics, and from the signs in front, one might even purchase tours.

The children will love this.

He found his uncle talking to some of the men. "Find out how much it would be to rent this place."

"The whole place?"

"Yeah."

"For how long?"

How long would the city be in an uproar? Acevedo couldn't bring the children back to the city until it was safe for them. "A couple of weeks should be long enough."

His uncle nodded and left.

The very dark brown man approached. He held a lit cigarette in one hand and gestured with it as he spoke. "Why are you here, Spadros? You look like a librarian."

"Close. I teach in a private school. Bridges history."

"So why are you leading a war?"

It took a moment for Acevedo to come up with an answer. "What's going on outside the fence became personal. The thought that this man would murder children —"

"Children die all the time. So you sign a petition, write a letter, like all the other good little citizens. Why are you trying to stage a coup over it?"

Acevedo couldn't answer.

Finally the man said, "**That's** why I don't trust you, Spadros. You may know what you're doing, but you don't know why, and that makes you dangerous. I'll help fight your war, because I see how it benefits my people. But don't expect anything from us after." He turned and left.

That was odd, Acevedo thought. *The man didn't even offer his name.* But his question was a valid one.

Why **am** I doing this?

Acevedo thought about it all the way home, and never could find a suitable answer.

***

Charlie was talking so fast Crispin could hardly follow him. "Slow down, pal. What did they say?"

His brother took a deep breath. "The King killed the King! And now he wants to kill us too, outside here. And they want to kill him! They want us to help, and we get to loot all we want."

Crispin wasn't totally clear on it, but he got the picture. "So what do you think?"

That finally slowed Charlie down some. "Like I told them, I don't see why we wouldn't. We got no stake in that so-called 'Pot of Gold.' I say piss on it, grab all we can. They got food, clothing, parts, lumber. We could use that stuff here, get everyone houses, like ours. And I was thinking:

why not grab the racetrack too? With all those horses, we could get around really well."

Crispin frowned. "That's on the other side of the city."

"But we'll have all the horses! All the rich folk put their horses to board there."

Crispin felt astonished. How did Charlie know that?

Charlie laughed. "I was talking with one of the guys from over there, and he said it. They got the same idea, but they're gonna grab it after the fight. I say we grab it right away. Then we can ride around the city all we want, and no one'll be able to stop us. They'll all be on foot." He paused. "We'll have all we need to make it work. Horses, food for them, place for them to stay —"

Charlie stopped, and Crispin could see the gears turning. When Charlie got that look on his face, something great was going to come out of it.

"One day the war's gonna end," Charlie said. "People are gonna wanna have fun." He grinned. "They'll pay good money to see our horses run again."

November 27th

Xavier crouched behind the door. He pulled a lever, one of a hundred spread throughout the training building.

The lever turned on the buzzer outside. It buzzed for thirty seconds, then stopped. Xavier listened as men crept closer, burst into the room, moved ahead.

He threw a small beanbag at the back of Varkonyi's head. "You're dead."

Groans filled the room.

"You didn't even look behind the door! It's not just Varkonyi. You all need to do better than this. Once they figure out what's going on, they won't be shooting beanbags at you." Xavier paused. "Come on, let's try it again."

Ocho Malize was having much better luck with his five. "Those guys are scary good," Malize said after the exercise. "Too bad they're completely nuts. Totally amoral. I had them fire on boards with their mothers' portraits on them and not one even hesitated." He paused. "What are you going to do with these guys?"

Xavier had an idea but he didn't want to say it yet. "You're doing great, Ocho. Just keep working with them. You'll see."

Xavier fell into bed once he got home from training. Between training his men half the day and standing guard all night, he felt exhausted much of the time. Even though

Kerr's men shadowed him constantly, Polansky Kerr refused to allow him to step down from his guard post, saying it would disturb the men. Because he had limited time to train them, most of his men were coming in on their time off to participate. *We're all tired, and tired men make mistakes.*

Perhaps Kerr intended it that way.

What was the man really planning? What did he hope to gain by this massacre?

***

When Acevedo got home from work, as usual, Papa sat at the kitchen table reading the paper. This time, though, Papa put the paper down. "Take a look at this."

Acevedo sat across from his father and read:

HOUSING PRICES FALL 5%

Southwest Quadrant Sell-Off

The Office of Housing reported today that housing prices fell 5% in the past month. On studying the data, the cause appears to be the large number of houses sold in the Southwest Quadrant.

When homeowners were questioned as to their reason for selling at this time, many cited the turmoil in the city. "I just don't feel safe here anymore," Sikelela Ikhadi Diamond told this reporter. "We're moving to the countryside."

A request for comment from the Office of the King was denied.

"Diamond," Acevedo said, remembering Jack's surgery apprenticeship. "I've heard that name before."

"One of the clans," Papa said. "They have very dark skin. Good looking, especially the women."

"Do they live in the Southwest Quadrant?"

"I think so." He paused. "Yeah. A big group of them live there. They're real quiet, stick to themselves."

This was very odd. Acevedo remembered the dark-skinned man at the meeting.

I don't trust you, Spadros.

"Is Uncle Vinny here?"

"I'm here," a voice came from way back in the house. A few minutes later, Uncle Vinny came in. "Whatcha need?"

"Who was the Diamond guy at the meeting?"

His uncle thought for a minute. "Name's Caesar, I think. Don't know him well. Why?"

Acevedo handed over the paper. "I think I may have unnerved him."

Uncle Vinny read it over, then nodded. "It's a good strategy. Pull the gentlefolk out of harm's way — then it doesn't matter who you hit or what you break." He laughed. "They're even making money with it." He put the paper down. "As long as they don't tip off the King, they can do whatever the hell they want." He ambled off back to where he came from.

"Papa," Acevedo said, "we're going to have to move too."

Papa smiled. "You finally figured that out. Me and your Mama talked about it the night Vincenzo came to me. We've been here a long time, but it's time to move on. Even if this works, who wants to live in a war zone? And if it doesn't, we won't be welcome here."

If we lose, Polansky Kerr's going to want our heads. "Where will we go?"

"Oh, we have a place out in the country — remember? We went there one summer when you were a boy."

Acevedo nodded. It was when he was twelve. "We own that? I thought it belonged to Granpa and Gramma."

"It did, and when they died, it belonged to me. Haven't been there in years, but it shouldn't take too long to get the place aired out and dusted. I'll have your sisters do it."

"Good gods, how much money do you have? Where

does it come from?"

Papa smiled. "I have enough." He leaned back in his chair. "Have you ever been to the casino?"

The question disoriented him. *The casino?* "No, I don't like to gamble."

Papa shrugged. "We have a deal with them. We get half their take every month, and we don't bother them."

Acevedo stared at his father, appalled. "That's extortion!"

"My son is so learned. He knows the meaning of so many words." He leaned forward. "Acevedo, listen to me. I'm the head of the Business. It's what we do. You might say it's a family tradition. You can learn to live with it or not. I want to give this all to you someday. But I'll give it to Vinny or one of your brothers if you're not comfortable taking care of the Family."

"I always thought you were joking when you said things like this," Acevedo said. "I never thought it was real." Then he had a horrible thought. "Where are the Bluffs?"

"In their rooms," Papa said. "Are you ashamed of what we do? Of what you're doing now? Meeting with criminals, plotting to overthrow the government?" He paused. "Because if you are, you should stop."

No, Acevedo thought. "That's different."

Papa shrugged. "You're going to hurt more people in a few months than I have my entire life. You need to figure out why it's okay for you to do what you're doing and not okay for me to do what I do." He picked up the paper and began reading.

This sounded too close for comfort to what Caesar Diamond had said.

*Why **am** I doing this?*

December 9th

Since Polansky Kerr's men seemed to be running the place, Xavier gave the men their 21 days off for Yuletide. Like every Yuletide, each of them was assigned on one of those days to patrol duty outside the palace grounds.

Before they left for the holidays, he met with each group again, except, of course his "top" group: they had no reason to be silent.

"This will be difficult. Your families will want to know what you're doing, why you've been working so many hours, what you think of the King. One wrong word could cause all our deaths. Be cautious."

His men agreed to keep quiet.

"See you January 4th," he said.

Ocho Malize said, "Anything you need me to do?"

"No, Ocho, go home and relax. Spend time with your family. I need you fresh when we return; we'll have a lot of work to do."

***

Acevedo released his students for Yuletide, and Jack came to his desk. "We'd be pleased to have you for Yuletide Center," he said. "It's my dad's birthday."

"A winter child!" Acevedo said. "So am I."

It was an old tradition from just after the Catastrophe: those born in the dark days from vernal to spring equinox celebrated at Yuletide Center, December 21st. Those born in the bright days from spring to vernal equinox celebrated on Midsummer's Day, June 21st.

Acevedo said, "My family will want me home that day. Perhaps the next?"

Jack beamed. "That would be great!"

***

Crispin Hartmann and his brother Charlie lay on the hills over the racetrack. Crispin peered through the binoculars they found in the trash.

The more Crispin thought about Charlie's idea, the more he liked it. This building was huge, it had fence all around it, and it was fairly defensible, especially with guys holding these hills. You could see someone coming for miles. The fact that they could get up here and this close without anyone even noticing was encouraging.

"We don't want to damage the complex," Crispin said. "But we have to get in and hold it."

Charlie rolled onto his side. He'd tried looking through the binoculars, but he said they made his eyes hurt. ""Can you see any guards?"

"Nope."

Charlie rolled back onto his stomach, put his chin on his folded arms. "We have to assume there's guards. Or security of some kind. Horses are expensive."

"But they probably won't have a lot of guns. They don't want the horses hurt. They just want to make sure no one steals them."

Charlie frowned. "How would they steal them? There must be a back gate. You see it?"

Crispin squinted. "No."

"It's got to be there. How do they get deliveries? How do they get new horses? We find the gate, we find the guards."

"Well, I don't see it. Maybe it's on the other side."

Charlie scooted back away from the peak and stood, dusting himself off. "We better get going, then. The sun's not going to be up all day."

Crispin laughed. "The sun **is** going to be up all day. That's what day means."

"Shut up. You know what I mean."

It took them a while to get back to the horses they stole and circle around. "Riding horses is hard," Crispin said. He could tell he was gonna be hurting tomorrow.

"Doesn't seem hard to me."

"You're so big that horse looks about ready to tip over."

"It's fine." Charlie patted the horse's neck. "I heard that they get foamy at the mouth when they're tired. His mouth looks good."

"Heh," said Crispin, "A cowboy as well as an Inventor."

Charlie seemed pleased with himself.

By the time they found a place to tie the horses and climbed up to the hills on the other side, the sun was low in the sky. But it shone right on the gate, and there were the men. "I see two men and a guard house," Crispin said. "There might be more inside."

Charlie nodded. "Sounds good. Let's go, before someone notices their horses are missing."

***

Blocker walked Wheelcard territory with a pad and pencil in hand. Where were the fences? Where were the walls? Where would they need to build barricades and where would they get the supplies for them?

Pretty much nothing happened during Yuletide — most shops were closed. The zeppelin only ran once a day. It would be hard to get anything shipped in until after the New Year.

But they could steal stuff.

Later that night, Blocker borrowed his brother's steam automobile and drove around in the rain looking for construction sites that weren't guarded.

He was looking at one when a guy walked right in front of him. Blocker slammed on the brakes. "Hey!"

A man came up to his window; Blocker rolled it down. "You lost?" Then the man laughed. "Blocker Goolsby. I might have known. You wouldn't be looking for something to steal, now, would you?"

"Not at all," Blocker said.

"You got a mighty nice automobile here. It'd be a pity if something were to happen to it."

"It's not mine, so I need to go return it."

The man gestured with his chin, and the other man moved away from the front of the car. "Go return it then. But if I see it again I might not be so nice next time."

Blocker got out of there as fast as he could, but not before a big chunk of mud went splat! on the back of his brother's car.

December 21st

Acevedo let out a contented sigh. After eleven days of parties, food, and drinking you'd think it would get repetitive, but it never did.

The room was full of his friends and family. He had his feet up on an ottoman, a drink in his hand, and here came the birthday cake. Half of his family were winter children, and so was Katherine, so there was lots of cake to go round.

Plus ten days of Yuletide still to come.

His little neice Donna came up to him. "Uncle Acevedo, would you tell me a story?"

"Don't bother your uncle Acevedo," his sister Cirulla said. "It's his birthday."

"It's my birthday too," she replied. "I want a story."

He put down his cake and drink. "Come here, sweet girl," Acevedo said, taking her onto his lap. "What story do you want?"

Donna said, "Bellicola and the Dragon."

"Ah, that's a good one."

His brother Cavallo, sitting next to him in another chair, glanced over. "You'll make a good father one day."

Cavallo was just two years younger than Acevedo, but he had eight children. His oldest son Roman was twenty and getting married soon.

Acevedo looked down at the little girl nestled in his

arms, and he held her close, feeling a great surge of affection for her.

Since Liza's death, he'd never even considered if he might be a good father. But now? *Maybe I would.*

***

The Cathedral hummed with activity — lines of families bringing children for their Blessing, food cooking for the feasts, gift exchanges in the back room.

Helena stood in the doorway to the vast main hall, surveying what the Dealer wrought.

Yuletide: A bountiful windfall to strengthen us to face the winter to come.

Activity on all fronts had quieted. Several thousand had been turned out of their homes right before Yuletide, yet the expected outcry never appeared.

Reports showed these exiles were widows, elderly, solitary people who had been living alone for years. Most were without family or friends to either help or wonder where they had gone.

We failed them.

The Dealers should have identified these people and at least offered the women an invitation to join them. But it was too late now.

Helena returned to her office and added outreach to the women in these camps into her planning.

Every bit of the Cathedral's resources had gone into building the new aid stations; another fifteen would be completed soon. Fortunately the police took the new status of their buildings in stride, and had offered no violence.

Helena smiled. The police didn't want to follow the King's orders either — which was encouraging.

The Dealers were her sisters, but also her charge, the gift the gods had given her to care for.

She and her advisors had gone over and over her plan, and it was sound. At least some of the Dealers would survive, no matter what happened, and more importantly, Bridges would be kept safe.

In the end, one person's life meant nothing, even her own. Protecting the city was all that mattered.

***

Crispin was busy in his metal office. Almost a thousand new insiders meant his camp was full to bursting, and the newcomers were outraged, angry, anguished, even after eleven days of exile.

He didn't blame them. Their people had betrayed them, and it was a bitter draught to swallow.

His cousin Shuli came in. "We put down a fight over by the fence."

"Put them to work building the base for the ray cannon."

Shuli, as big as Charlie but with the same straight black hair as Crispin's, let out an amused laugh and left.

Shuli wouldn't go anywhere; they had runners to every part of their territory.

Charlie had set that up long ago. One runner to loiter in an area to get the news, another nearby to send it out again. Between them and the army of children scampering for ways to get an extra roll in their bellies, Crispin knew everything that happened almost as soon as it happened.

Charlie stepped in, about filling the doorway. "I just thought of something."

Crispin, about to start melting lead again, felt startled. Charlie almost never came down here. "What?"

"It's gonna be hard, defending there and here both."

Crispin nodded. Charlie had become obsessed with the racetrack, never stopped talking about it.

"So we gotta move there."

"What? We gotta house **here**, Charlie!"

"Listen to me. Yeah, we gotta house here. But the racetrack has a huge building! You said ten stories —"

"The front, yeah. No way to tell how much of that you can live in."

"But we can make it livable. And it's gotta have all that fancy stuff for their guests. Just imagine — inside plumbing, running water, a real kitchen for Nana." He paused for a moment. "Besides, I can build them another house anywhere they want, a better one."

"You wanna just leave all these people?"

"Naw, bring them with us! I mean, after we get all the stuff we want. It'll be great. We send them off — get all the stuff you want, bring it to us. I had another idea — grab all the carts, too!"

The carts. Crispin stared at his brother, astonished, awestruck. What an idea!

"We'll have the horses, the carts, damn, get the carriages too, if we can. Bring it all to the racetrack. By the end of this we'll have all the stuff we need."

Crispin considered the matter. "We gotta figure out what to do with the people who won't fight. Some are old; we'll need a way to move them."

"Won't know how many that'll be until it comes down to it," Charlie said. "Just walking down here I saw an old lady yelling for a shotgun and some shells to plug those Kerr men who dragged her outside."

Crispin laughed. "On Yuletide Center! Well, I guess you're right; we'll see. Do you know how to make carts?"

"I can probably figure it out. Let me ask around — there might be a cartmaker in all this."

Charlie lumbered off, and Crispin sat, his mind reeling. Actually move? He'd lived his whole life here.

But if he could make a better life for these people, this was too good an opportunity to pass up.

January 4th

Acevedo passed out the syllabus for this month's reading. Everyone was present, and he felt relieved to see them healthy and safe.

"I hope you had a pleasant holiday," he said, and Jack grinned. They had a good time on his visit, and Acevedo was glad to see Xavier's father again after so many years. "It's time to get back to work."

The class groaned, some throwing themselves on their desks as if despondent, but it was all in good fun.

"This month, we're going to discuss the political changes in Bridges during the seventeenth century." He pulled out his notes. "Please open your books to chapter ten."

***

Blocker walked his streets again. He'd gotten less conspicuous men — and some of the older boys — to "borrow" a great deal of sand, which they carted off and began filling cotton feedbags with. He had the little kids running around searching for old nails. They'd pound those into thin boards and make spiked gates and various traps for the areas they couldn't defend directly. And a shipment of guns and ammo was on its way.

People strolled along. It was all peaceful, without a hint of what was coming. Would it be better to tell them?

But where would they go?

Blocker was afraid of something else. The more people that knew about this, the higher the chance someone would squeal. That could get them all killed. Sooner or later crazy old Kerr would turn on them — and all the gangs — as part of "cleaning up the city."

If Kerr finds out about this too soon, I'll find my head in someone's sights.

Blocker glanced around, shuddering.

Calm yourself. No one knows yet.

But there were too many windows on this street for his liking. He had to make sure everyone knew what was going on the day it happened, so his men didn't find themselves shot from behind by a frightened neighbor.

What was that Spadros said? The guards would wear white armbands to identify themselves. A good idea.

Blocker turned and went to a guy he knew who sold cloth. He was sure they could work something out.

February 17th

Acevedo passed out forms for a field trip.

"Since so many of you wanted to know how the dome was built, I've arranged for you to visit a science museum to learn all the details."

The class burst into excited chatter.

"Bring back these forms by Monday so I can arrange transportation. Your whole family is welcome — just indicate on the form how many people will be coming. Since it's so far in the countryside, it'll be an overnight trip, so bring bed rolls. Also bring a picnic lunch for when we arrive. We'll provide the rest of the food."

The children stared at him in amazement.

"It doesn't cost anything?" Jack said.

"It's all been taken care of," Acevedo said.

Being in a crime family certainly had its advantages. Papa was paying for the entire thing.

"All right," Acevedo said. "Quiet, please. Let's get started. Open your books to chapter fourteen."

***

Helena sat reading a report of unusual Guard activity prior to Yuletide: extra shifts at odd hours, with almost 100% attendance.

With the recent orders from the King they had intercepted, she expected a rash of resignations, not this.

"Get me the files on this Guard commander, Alcatraz," she called out.

He must be a persuasive man.

Or he was planning something.

"Yes, Director," her assistant Octavia said.

A few moments later, Octavia came in bearing a folder.

Helena read what they had on the man. Received the Dealer's Blessing at age eight. High marks in school. Widowed, two teenage children. Assigned to the throne room for nine years.

So he knew the old king well.

Present in the throne room during the assassination.

What really happened there that night?

The list of known associates included his son's high school teacher, who Mr. Alcatraz had been corresponding frequently with in the past few weeks, a man named Acevedo Spadros.

Helena's assistant Octavia came in. "I just received a collated report from several stations outside the fence. It seems the criminal groups are having meetings. Very secretive ones, too. I'm not sure what it means."

Spadros. That name sounded familiar.

"Give me the report. And get me a list of all the criminal factions in Bridges."

"Yes, Director."

It took an hour for Octavia to pull together the several lists of known criminal groups. But once Helena went through it all, she laughed. *The audacity!*

"What is it?" Octavia said. "What have you learned?"

Helena put her elbows on her desk, suddenly sobered at the ramifications. This was going to change everything. "Call a general meeting. I want everyone there."

"All the Dealers?"

"Every single one in the city. Prepare the Cathedral."

"Anything else?"

"Assign a surveillance team to Acevedo Spadros. I want to know where he goes and when."

"The schoolteacher? I had him for Bridges History."

Interesting. "Tell me about him."

Octavia sat. "A kind man. Honest, appreciative of truth. Good with students. Knows history better than anyone I've ever met." The woman seemed a bit in awe.

Charismatic, as well.

"He's important in this." Helena said. "I mean him no harm. But something is happening, and I must know what."

If her hunch was correct, this was going to be a longer play than she ever imagined.

My great-grandchildren may curse me some day, Helena thought, *if I survive.*

***

Xavier watched his men train. They had done very well, learning how to enter a building, check the corners, move out, search each room before moving to the next.

They couldn't train in the Armory itself — that would be foolhardy — but he had them study the Armory's blueprints and changed the interior of the training building weekly to simulate each floor.

Ocho Malize came up to him and bowed. "The King wishes to see you, sir."

A spike of fear. "Very well. Take over here."

Xavier went to the King's office.

The King stood with his crown on, gazing out of the window at the practicing Guards.

"You wished to see me, Your Majesty?"

Polansky Kerr turned to face him. "Indeed. Report."

"The training is progressing on schedule. We'll be ready to complete the mission on March 12 as requested."

"I've changed my mind. We attack March 1st, at dawn."

Xavier stared at Polansky Kerr in shock. That was less than two weeks away! "Your Majesty?"

"Do it. Dismissed."

February 20th

Acevedo paced in his room, furious. Damn! After all his efforts to get this to work, that madman decided to move up the schedule.

He had angry parents in the Headmaster's office who had taken two days off work for the excursion. Now the Headmaster was demanding to know who gave authorization for an overnight trip including young women.

Half a dozen gang leaders had sent marks of their displeasure at the changes, including one who left a pile of cow manure on his doorstep.

Papa sent Uncle Vinny to handle that one.

This was getting out of control. Too many people knew of the changed schedule, and that put Xavier directly into harm's way.

And the last of the ray cannon had been seized by the authorities in Azimoff!

We have seven of them. That should be enough.

He held a letter from the Diamond clan:

> You promised us equal entry to the city! Now you tell us the Diamonds will be denied their rightful spoils by refusing us a cannon.
>
> We will never forget this outrage. You are a betrayer, Spadros, of friends and foes alike. We will stop your Family's lust to dominate this city.

What we seize you will never take from us.
Caesar Diamond

Disgusted, Acevedo threw the letter on the floor.

A soft knock. "Come in."

Katherine opened the door. "I heard."

He didn't want to alarm her. "I wanted the children to be safe so badly. But now the Headmaster's said only girls accompanied by a parent may attend —"

She came to him, took his hands, and her touch warmed him. "Hush. You've done your best."

"I fear for them." Acevedo knew full well what happened to young girls during war, yet he didn't want to speak of such things. Not to her. "I want to talk to the parents, tell them the truth, beg them to attend —"

"No," Katherine said. "Your friend risked his life to bring us this new time. Parents have already gone to the Headmaster. What if one of these parents takes the truth to the King?"

She was right. But it ate at him. "I wish I could tell the whole city of their fate." He had a nightmare of the city awash with blood, full of ruins, his students lying dead.

Her face hardened. "This city chose its fate when it put up that fence."

Such words from her shocked him.

"This city is cruel," she said. "Heartless. And from what Molly tells me, it didn't begin that way. What changed?"

Acevedo had studied history all his life, but the question surprised him. "We lost who we were." He pointed to his heart. "In here. Became afraid." He felt very still inside, like the calm before a storm. "A man asked why I'm doing this, and I don't have an answer."

She smiled. "You're doing this because you haven't lost who you are," she laid her hand on his chest. "In here."

He took her hand in both of his and kissed it.

Gods, she's beautiful.

His mouth went dry; his body yearned to move closer. He gripped her hand, squeezed his eyes shut in desperation.

"Please tell me you're here why I think you're here."

"Acevedo," his father said from the doorway, startling him. "It's late. Mrs. Bluff, you should leave."

Color flushed her cheeks. "My apologies, sir. Good night." She hurried out past Papa.

Rage and humiliation. "Close the door and go," Acevedo said bitterly, turning away.

"I feared this would happen when you brought her," Papa said. "What are your intentions towards this woman?"

I want her. I need her. I barely know her. "I don't know."

"As I thought. I'm sorry, son — we should have arranged a marriage for you long before this. Twenty-five years is too long for a man to be alone."

Acevedo had never felt alone, until now.

February 27th

Octavia ran up as Helena headed to the general meeting.

"Whatever's happening, the date has changed," Octavia panted. "I'm getting reports from all over the city, including something about a field trip Spadros is on being changed. March 1st." She stared at Helena. "Is this what I think it is?"

Helena smiled, but her heart wasn't in it. "Let me know after the meeting."

Helena entered the vast Cathedral, the center of all power, and felt dwarfed by the building, the responsibility, the awesome duty she had to Bridges.

I must keep my city safe, no matter what the cost.

But her hands shook with fear.

No seat, no pew sat empty, no inch of floor. Women sat on each other's laps, the floor, the window-sills. Women crowded in the doorway. Everyone was here.

Helena remembered the day she lay bleeding on the doorstep there, after being beaten by her husband.

But I didn't go back.

Before, she had always gone back. But that time, she didn't, not even when he stood at the doorstep there and pleaded with her.

And now, thirty years later, she stood here.

I won't go back on my word out of fear, or false hope. No, not ever again.

Helena moved to the podium.

"My beloved sisters, today is a day of mourning. Not for our King, or for our way of life, or even for our morality, but for the promise Benjamin Kerr envisioned when he built Bridges: a garden city of peace. We have failed him.

"He of all men understood men's hearts. Benjamin Kerr understood what would happen if evil men ruled his city. We need not speak of it.

"I thank you for your kind words, and I thank you for your service to this city. That service will never end so long as the Dealers remain.

"We must each choose how we will serve. I know some of you joined the Dealers to engage in quiet solitude, others to escape abuse, still others to serve the poor. Each of us will find our resolve tested in ways we know not. And the time for you to choose is now."

The women murmured in confusion.

"Civil war is coming." *There, I said it plainly.* "Men will come to the Cathedral to mine its riches. I will not let the city of Bridges fall into their hands."

Everyone sat up. The room fell silent.

They know exactly what I mean, Helena thought, and the thought excited her. The brave, smart women she led gave her great pride.

"Here is your choice: to stay, or to scatter outside the fence. There will be no half-measure. Staying will mean death, or worse. Scattering means exile, and a lifetime of service. You must not let the Dealers die. Remember the Dealer's love as you make your choice. Either choice requires strength and courage. Let no one forget it."

She took a deep breath. "Our time has run out. You must choose now, today, at once. Pick a Station and go to it, or collect your things and return here. Tell no one. The future of this city lies in your hands now. It has been a great honor to serve you."

She raised her hand, ignoring the sobs filling the room. "The Dealer's Blessing upon you."

"And also on you."

Helena turned to look at the altar, a flat sandstone rectangle eight feet long, four feet wide, and as high as her waist. *Floorman help us both.*

She went into her office, and Octavia followed.

A bust of Benjamin Kerr stood there, as well as one of Athena Stronghold, first Director of Bridges.

What would they have done?

"You must go with them," Helena said. "You are Director now. May your reign be long and happy."

Octavia said nothing, and after a while, Helena heard the door close behind her.

An hour later, Helena went back to the hall, fearing it might remain empty. Sixty-three women sat in the front rows: plain and beautiful, old and young, tall and short, some she had never met.

Helena sat on the steps before them, and put her elbows on her knees. "I am no longer Director; I'm just a woman like you. But I have a few words of comfort left." She took a deep breath. "From this day forth, we are dead."

The women looked at each other with concern.

"Dead women don't care what happens to them. They are simply bodies. They don't reveal secrets. They neither betray their sisters nor their city. We are dead."

The women nodded, faces sober as they began to understand what she meant. "We are dead."

"From this day forward, we are loved. Women who are loved, give love, in whatever way is needed."

Their faces softened. They began to understand her plan. "We are loved."

Helena smiled. *Sixty-three women. It might be enough.*

"Oh beloved dead, let's make a feast to celebrate our last nights in Bridges."

The women cheered.

February 28th

A long line of carriages waited in front of the school when Xavier went to see his children off on their trip. "It sounds like a grand adventure," Xavier said.

Xavier thought the idea of a field trip to get the children out of the city a stroke of genius — until Joy was refused admittance for not having a parent attend with her.

"I have work tonight," he said. "Her brother is with her. Is that not suitable?"

"It is not," the Headmaster said. "Unless you find a proper chaperone for the girl, she may not attend."

Xavier searched frantically for a solution, but could find none. He hadn't asked his father to go on the trip, and now his father was on his way to the zeppelin station, having decided to seek his fortune in another city. Xavier had nowhere for Joy to go, no family in the countryside.

How could he do this if his daughter was home alone in the midst of war?

"If I take care of her, would that be sufficient?"

The woman who he'd seen after the parent conference came up. "My daughter is on the trip. I'd be willing to supervise the girl."

Xavier looked to the Headmaster.

"Very well," he said. "Being as you are a Guard, and a parent is willing to take your place, I'll let the girl attend."

"Thank you," Xavier said, relieved.

At least now his children might survive this.

***

Acevedo was pleased with how the trip was going so far. He had to get out and talk to the men at the gate, but that was a minor detail. They just wanted to know where he was going with all these people, and when they'd be back.

After that, they passed a quarter mile of tents and lean-tos, then some ramshackle huts for another quarter mile, then the buildings became more substantial. The sheer number of people living outside the fence astonished him.

The buildings turned to fields, which turned to farms and small villages. The horses trotted along.

It seemed a pleasant day.

Katherine sat as far away as one might in a carriage, and had said nothing to him since the embarrassment of the night before.

Acevedo didn't know whether to be angry at his father for humiliating her or angry at her for being in his room.

Finally, he decided not to be angry at anyone. It was his own fault for allowing her to stay there.

What did he feel for her?

She was comely, a good mother, had taken on a great deal of the housework since arriving, and had good instincts. The way she stepped in to help Xavier with his daughter was commendable.

But do I want to marry her?

Part of him couldn't think of anything else.

I am not going to my uncle for this again, he thought.

Uncle Vinny had gotten him evening encounters with his "ladies," but Acevedo always felt as if he'd made the wrong decision afterwards. And there was always the fear of the wrong person seeing him — if word got out, he could lose his job, or worse, his standing.

No more. Papa was right; he needed to marry. It had been long enough.

He would become an instant father to Molly. *Am I ready*

for that?

Yet Katherine was young enough that they might have children of their own.

Acevedo thought of Liza, her still pale face as he held her, and he turned away from the others in the carriage. *Perhaps I don't have to decide anything now.*

Once this was all over —

Then what?

This surprised him. What would they do, once they had captured the King? Would one of his sons take over?

What if the sons were worse than the father?

I can't believe we didn't think about this.

It was out of Acevedo's hands. Now that he had rescued these children and their parents, he wouldn't leave them. Whatever decisions were made there on Market Center were up to Xavier Alcatraz to make.

*****

Xavier stood in front of his "elite" group of five in the morning sun. "I have one last training for you. It's the most difficult task I could come up with, but I have every expectation that you will succeed. If you can accomplish this, you'll receive a special commendation, plus the reward of your choice. Anything you want.

"Meet in front of the Armory at 0200 tomorrow, and Malize will give you your orders. Think about it, write down what you want, and hand it in then."

They replied, "Yes, sir!"

Xavier didn't trust anyone but himself to give these orders, but he couldn't chance it that one of these men might report to the King. They and Polansky Kerr were too similar in disposition for his liking.

Next were the rounds of training with his various groups. To each he repeated their mission, emphasized that this was treason and they would hang if they failed. "If any of you don't think you can do this, I'll dismiss you to your homes now. If your families have somewhere to go in the countryside, I suggest you send them there. If our mission doesn't succeed, this could get ugly."

His men nodded, and a few decided to leave.

"I should have taken the resignation instead of this," one said. "I can't betray the man I swore to serve."

"Noted," Xavier said. "Your resignation is accepted. You've been a brave Guardsman and a loyal friend. If you betray us, though, we'll be forced to kill you."

Shock rippled through the room as each man realized what was happening.

"This is real," another said.

"Yes, it is," Xavier said. "Unfortunately, we've been left with little choice."

***

When the carriages reached the facility, Uncle Vinny stood out front waiting. Papa had sent him ahead to secure the building, but Acevedo's uncle didn't look happy. "We found all the scientists dead."

Acevedo stared at his uncle in shock.

"It's a huge fucking mess. Your brothers are cleaning it up, but it's going to take a while."

"Any sign who did it?"

"I dunno. It could be anyone from one of those guys at the meeting to the King himself."

"The King?" That seemed alarming.

Uncle Vinny looked grim. "I wouldn't put anything past that man. Why he'd kill them, I have no idea. A warning?"

"Can we get a message to Xavier?"

"We can try."

Acevedo turned to the group, who had all gotten out of their carriages, "They're not ready for us yet. Let's eat."

He led them to a grassy field past the building with trees past that, and the families began to spread blankets and open their baskets.

Then he went to his father and told him the news.

"I knew something was wrong when I saw Vincenzo out front. He hates just standing around."

Dark stains lay on the ground, and Scoop began licking

one. "Stop that," Papa said, kicking sand over the stain. He tugged at the dog's leash. "Come on."

Mama came up with their basket. "I'm ready to eat. Where do you want to sit?"

Acevedo felt ill. "Anywhere's fine."

People ate, sat under parasols, talked. The children began playing on the grass, running, wrestling. Acevedo wondered what they would do if they knew there were a dozen dead inside.

Mama came over and sat beside him. "Are you well? You're not eating."

"I have a lot on my mind."

"Mrs. Bluff told me what happened last night," she said. "She's a fine woman."

This was high praise from her. Most women weren't good enough for any of them. "What makes you say that?"

"Acevedo!" Mama seemed scandalized.

"I don't mean it that way, Mama. I just want to know what you think of her. The truth. I want to hear it from you."

His mother peered at him, nodding slowly. "Well, she's devout: she and Molly pray the Four Corners every day. She works hard — I've hardly had to do anything since she arrived. She does all the cooking, the cleaning —"

"Wait. She's been cooking, too?" The food had tasted just like Mama's.

"She asked me how I made things. She's a quick learner, that one."

Acevedo felt astonished.

"And," Mama said, "she sees the good in people. I think she'd make a good wife for you."

Acevedo smiled. "Mama —" He leaned over and kissed his mother's cheek. "Her husband's barely been in the ground six months. Shouldn't I give her some time before I start booking the chapel?"

"Maybe you should ask **her** that," Mama said.

Acevedo turned to find Katherine watching them, and he smiled at her. "Maybe I will."

***

It was another hour before Uncle Vinny came out and told them the coast was clear.

Acevedo stood and called out to the crowd. "If you'd like to take the tour now, they're ready."

A flurry of collecting baskets, folding blankets, and picking up various lost items commenced. After everything was put back into the carriages, the tour began.

The tour guides were among the dead, but Acevedo's brother Cavallo volunteered to guide the tour. "Come right this way, single file."

The children eagerly studied the various displays, chattering amongst themselves, debating over some point or another, and rushing in groups to Cavallo for the answer.

After one such group left, Acevedo said, "I'm astonished at your knowledge of the subject."

Cavallo grinned. "I just go with whatever seems most reasonable. I have no idea what the real answer is."

Acevedo said. "Give my congratulations to Roman. Make sure they know where to meet us."

Cavallo's son and daughter-in-law, gone in Italy these six weeks, sent a message from their honeymoon: they were expecting a child.

Even though Acevedo knew in his mind they would get home safely, he didn't think he would feel at rest until he saw them back home.

Cavallo smiled. "They'll be fine."

The shadows were lengthening outside by the time the tour completed, and good smells wafted through the room. "Out to the courtyard," Cavallo said.

One of Acevedo's brothers turned an entire sheep on a rotisserie, and Acevedo's sisters-in-law came out bearing platters of food, which they put on a long table.

The chairs had been placed around small square tables, which were now set. In the center of the courtyard stood an unlit bonfire.

This time, Acevedo was hungry, and he set to his meal

with relish, earlier events forgotten.

The bonfire was lit, accompanied by songs and dancing. Then the carriages were unloaded before putting the children to bed in the large rooms on either side of the building: the girls in the far room, the boys near the front entrance.

Some of the older adults went to bed then, but the rest sat watching the fire, sipping wine and talking.

Acevedo moved to a table near the gate, where he might see the sky over the island. He didn't think he would be able to sleep.

Uncle Vinny came to his table. "We're leaving. The boys and I have the real work now."

Uncle Vinny and Acevedo's brothers would take the seven carriages. They were to transport and supervise the seven ray cannon, to make sure they didn't fall into anyone else's hands. Papa paid a **lot** of money for them.

"Best of luck," Acevedo said. "My blessings go with you. Watch your back."

Uncle Vinny grinned. "I always do."

Acevedo found a half-full wine bottle and returned to his table, only to find Katherine sitting there. "I suppose I should ask if I might join you," he said, "but it seems wrong way round."

She smiled. "I don't mean to intrude on your solitude; I hoped you wished to share it."

I could have a worse companion tonight. "As a matter of fact, I do."

***

After night court, Polansky Kerr said, "I hear you've had some resignations today."

"Just men who don't wish to carry out our mission. We don't need their kind here."

From the corner of his eye, Xavier saw a grin spread over Polansky Kerr's face. "You're exactly right. I want their names. After we're done tomorrow, they'll be executed."

For resigning their commission? "Your Majesty?"

"You heard me. I want their names. On my desk. Tonight."

"Yes, Your Majesty."

What a madhouse this has become, Xavier thought, as he placed the list on Kerr's desk. Without even inquiring as to why the men resigned, Polansky Kerr was ready to execute his most faithful Guards.

His assistant Peter Moysian was still at his desk when Xavier went to his office. Xavier wrote some letters, then called Peter in. "Send these summons at once."

The man carried a medium sized box with a letter on top. "Sir, a package has arrived. And a message."

Taking out a knife, Xavier opened the box: white armbands. "Excellent! These are for the training exercise tonight. You're to distribute one to each of the men as they report for duty."

"Yes, sir."

The message was from Mr. Spadros.

All the scientists were dead?

Xavier didn't know what it meant. Polansky Kerr didn't seem any different from his usual; if he knew of their plans, they should be dead by now.

Xavier went to his assigned post outside the royal bedchambers, glancing at Ocho Malize.

The man seemed nervous. Xavier felt the same.

***

Blocker had knocked on every door of his territory in the last six hours. His throat hurt, his feet hurt, and he felt exhausted. But his efforts had gotten them another fifty-odd men who agreed to help defend their turf, and he had three dozen women cooking and a bunch of kids storing water in case the power went out.

He told them all to go to their basements if they got too scared. "It's set up with blankets and food," he said.

An old man said, "You've done well for us, Blocker. I used to wonder about you Wheelcard boys, but now that we're in need, you've made us proud."

Blocker didn't know what to say. He and Fish had run around with the Wheelcards since he was five.

Never thought anyone'd be proud of us.

Just wait until Fish hears about this!

***

Crispin Hartmann was casting the last of the bullets when Shuli came in.

"Scouts are back. The west bridges are completely blocked. We can't go that way."

Crispin frowned. This made no sense. "Why would they block the bridges?"

"No idea, but they cursed at the scouts when they asked. A bunch of big guys with real dark skin."

"How about to the north?"

"Outside the fence? Those bridges are still clear."

"Make sure they stay clear. And get the men going. We have to get to that racetrack before anyone else does."

Shuli turned to send the runners. Then he came back in. "Charlie and Wànzi went with them."

"Good. Did the guy with the ray cannon get here yet?"

"Yeah. A Spadros. I showed him where to set up."

"Great." Crispin got up, went to the door.

The night was clear, with no moon. "Looks like a perfect night for a party."

March 1st

At the first calling of midnight, Xavier and Malize turned, strode to the beat of the chimes, and went through the first set of doors, the next set of men falling in behind them. Soon men met up from all corners of the palace, passing the darkened courtyard and moving in formation to the Armory, where the rest of the men stood waiting silently, their eyes on him.

Xavier moved the group to a spot he had selected weeks earlier, where no rifleman could shoot those on the ground from a building.

Xavier's assistant, Peter Moysian, handed armbands to him and the men behind him, then returned. "All present, sir, with the exception of team King."

Who were not expected until 0200.

Xavier took out his pocketwatch: 0035. "Very good. Mr. Moysian, you officially have the next two weeks off. You're ordered to go home, get your wife and children, and make for the Rim."

"Sir?"

"Use the main road. The Hotel Attitude on Rim Road, on the left, just before the train station is excellent — put the bill on my tab."

Moysian seemed shocked. "But sir —"

Xavier smiled. "You've been a fine assistant. I want you

to survive this. Now go."

"Yes, sir." The man turned and hurried off.

"That was kind of you, sir," Malize said.

"Just getting the innocents out of harm's way."

His assistant had worked double shifts for weeks not knowing what he worked on. Xavier refused to let the man — or his family — be hurt if he had any say in the matter.

Xavier raised his hands and signalled — One: Go.

The Armory infiltration group, 100 men led by Ocho Malize, moved to cover the front and back of the massive building, then begin the long process of destroying all the Kerr men inside.

Once the Armory was secured, Malize carried the red firework, which would be shot from the roof.

Two, Three, Four, Five: Go.

These men, fifty to a group, would cover the bridges, to keep anyone from entering or leaving the island. Each group would send a man back when they were in position. These groups had the farthest to travel.

Six: Go.

50 men to form a perimeter around the palace itself, preventing anyone from leaving or entering the building.

The clock tower struck one.

Faint "pop" noises of gunfire could be heard from inside the Armory. His men had encountered resistance.

If they or any of the other groups needed help, they had runners to send word, and the 45 men positioned around Xavier could be deployed to cover them.

Xavier wanted nothing more than to be in there with his men, but his place was out here, in relative safety. If anything went wrong, his men needed to know exactly where to find him.

Xavier took a deep breath. "Now we wait."

***

Acevedo and Katherine sat watching as the bonfire died down and collapsed, as the wine vanished, as one by one, people said good night.

106

Finally Papa came over to their table. "No way I'm gonna be able to sleep on a night like this, even if I could leave the two of you out here alone." He let out a short laugh. "You want me here, or over there?"

Acevedo felt a great fondness for his old Papa. "Sit with us," he said. "This is your night, if it's anyone's. Without you, none of this would be happening."

Papa laughed. "Trapasso Spadros, Kingmaker. I doubt it'll be remembered that way."

Acevedo shrugged. "I just study history, I don't write it."

"You're writing it now, son. Everything we do is part of history. We just don't know it most times."

Papa took out a cigar and lit it, the glow matching the dying fire off to Acevedo's right. "Tonight'll be in a book someday, I can feel it."

The breeze blew warm for fall. The stars shone brightly over the darkened city; there were just a few lights visible here and there.

"Why are you doing this, Mr. Spadros?" Katherine said. "Why are you doing this? You're not poor, and we're safe enough. Why risk your life to get rid of this King?"

Suddenly, Acevedo had an answer. He put his hand on hers. "I think this is what I was meant to do."

A streak of red light lifted into the sky and exploded into a burst of red showers.

***

Helena sat on the roof with the other women and watched the red firework rise over the city.

That is the signal of our doom.

Helena rose. "Let's go downstairs and meet our fate."

The other women followed, hand in hand — some weeping, some stoic, some angry.

Helena understood; she had felt all those ways over the past few hours.

I can help them bear this.

Helena led them to the altar. "Let's make the Dealer's Oath one last time."

She and the other women came round the altar, placing their hands on it. It felt cool and smooth.

"We swear to defend you, Bridges," Helena said, "to the end of our lives."

"So be it."

"We swear to pass the sacred knowledge to our daughters, and our daughters alone."

"So be it."

"We swear to never reveal the secret of this place until the land is restored."

"So be it."

"We swear to never reveal the secret of this place without grave need."

"So be it."

"Only if the question is asked, the woman provided, and the room cleansed should the sacred Heart of Bridges ever be exposed."

"So we swear. May we suffer the Fire for our betrayal."

Helena let out a breath. "I don't know how long we have. Hours, days perhaps, certainly not more than a week. What shall we do?"

The youngest among them said, "Let us cast the Cards, and chart the future of our City, for as long as we can."

***

Xavier's pocket watch said 0145. "Move in."

The group moved past the entry guards into the front lobby, his men taking up positions at each window.

Xavier turned to the men standing guard at the first entry. "Get everyone but the ones covering the roof down here now."

Malize gave the order then watched as the men assembled. "Now what?"

"Follow me."

Xavier and the men from upstairs went outside. His "top" men were there early. "Very good."

He handed each of the five men an armband. "Your assignment is to infiltrate the palace and secure the King."

"I'll be right back," Malize said.

One of the five said, "We're to go into the royal bed-chambers itself?"

"Yes," Xavier said. "Bring the King here, alive, before 0300 hours. Kill anyone who tries to stop you."

He turned to the group from upstairs. "You're their support. Secure the palace, cover them if they need help."

The group of five pursed their lips, squinted at him. "This is no exercise," one said. "The reward of our choice?"

Xavier said, "Did you write it down?"

Xavier reached out his hand, and the men dug in their pockets, handing over scraps of paper.

One man's said, "Those women the King has."

Another's said, "Enough money to do what I want the rest of my life."

The third said, "I wanna live in the palace."

The fourth said, "My own private servants and villa out in the country."

The last one was blank.

Xavier was puzzled. "What do you want?"

The man said, "Didn't know until now. But I wanna kill the King. Whenever you do him in."

Xavier nodded. "Done."

"You didn't trust us," the first one said.

"No," Xavier said, "I didn't, but I do now." He gestured to the group of men behind him, who stood gaping at their exchange. "These men are yours to deploy as you will. I'd use them for securing the palace and fighting armed resistance; they haven't been trained the same as you have. You bring the King here alive before 0300, and you'll get everything you asked for."

Satisfied, the five men padded off without another word. After a moment's hesitation, the rest followed.

Xavier looked over the city. The night was dark, with no moon. The men should be able to make it there undiscovered. They had the perimeter and the bridges secured. There was no way for Polansky Kerr to escape.

The blue firework was in his pack. Should he light it?

No, I need to be sure we have him. I need to do this right.

Xavier wanted the King put on trial for his crimes. He wanted proof of the King's crimes presented and legal testimony from everyone involved. He wanted it all made public, so everyone knew why they did this.

And he needed to make sure this wasn't going to come back on his men. If the King somehow escaped, they would need help hunting down Kerr and his men, or none of them would ever be safe again.

Ocho Malize, now standing behind him, said, "You really gonna do all that?"

Xavier shrugged, shoving the papers into his pocket. "I'm not entirely sure they'll make it back with the King alive. But if they do, I'm a man of my word."

After a moment, Malize raised his voice. "Here he is. You said you'd let me see her."

Ten men came round the corner, crouched low against the wall, so the men at the windows couldn't fire on them. They were Kerr's men!

They dragged a bound, frightened, pregnant woman along with them. "Sure did," their leader said. "Now you finish the job."

Malize betrayed me.

They had his wife?

"I'm sorry, sir," Malize whispered, "there wasn't any other way."

Hot metal stabbed into Xavier's back, and he couldn't breathe. He felt himself fall.

Ocho Malize stood over him, waving a bloody knife. "He's dead." He turned to the windows. "Stand down."

Kerr's men leapt up, came towards him, leaving the woman by the wall.

Malize yelled, "Fire!"

The air filled with noise as men spun and fell around him. Malize was one of them, and his head lay on Xavier's chest. "Forgive me," he said, and closed his eyes.

Malize betrayed me.

I can't breathe.

A woman screamed.

Men began shouting, but Xavier didn't understand what they said.

"Tell my kids I love them," he tried to say, but he heard nothing come out.

He looked up. The night was very dark.

He pictured his children. *I love you.*

The sound of the bridges detonating was the last thing Xavier remembered.

***

"That's the signal!" Crispin yelled.

"I know," the Spadros man at the ray cannon said, turning the cannon to the right. "Keep your people back."

"Get back, get back!" Crispin waved them back as a Charlie-sized bolt of red flew diagonally to the fence, paused briefly, then flew past, everything burning in its wake.

"Good gods!" Crispin said, terrified of the thing's power.

"Nice," the man said.

Crispin screamed at the people on the left, who had moved forward to see the massive red-rimmed hole in the wrought-iron fence."Back! Back, you idiots!"

The man turned the cannon, and the people rushed back, now screaming in terror themselves. The man fired, and another hole appeared in the fence, the hedges, and everything down along the line.

Fires smouldered along the first line as the red rim around the hole faded to black.

Crispin had warned everyone that the metal would be hot even when it turned black, but some were moving to the fence on that side already. He turned to the Spadros man. "Do the middle hole and let's get this over with."

"Sure thing, boss," the man said.

This was too much weapon. Crispin felt afraid of the thing. "Get it out of here."

"My pleasure." The man turned it off.

People started grabbing sacks, weapons, anything they thought would help, and running for the holes.

"Move out, but carefully!" Crispin said. Smoke was rising for a half-mile off, and in the distance, all over the city.

What the hell had they done?

****

In the city, the blast from the exploding bridges shook the buildings all around Blocker and his men.

"They didn't catch the King," Blocker said. "Damn."

"We're in trouble," his brother Fish said.

People began turning on the lights, pouring out of their homes, asking what happened.

Blocker took a deep breath, let it out. "Yeah. Deep trouble." His throat was so sore he could barely talk. "Get these people back in their homes. And get everyone to turn off those lights. We gotta survive our pals coming to visit. We'll worry about the King later."

Nothing happened for several hours. Blocker climbed to the tallest building, but all he could see was what looked like smoke off towards the fence. A lot of smoke.

Fish had followed him up there. "Looks like they set things on fire."

Ray cannon. Blocker didn't know what that was, but if it could pierce iron bars thicker than his thumb, it could probably do a lot more.

****

Crispin sighed tiredly. Charlie had made thirty carts, but they still weren't enough. The camps to the east were full of people who'd been abandoned and wanted to go with them. They'd decided long ago to let as many as wanted join them. It seemed like a good situation all round.

"If you can walk, get out and let those that can't in," Crispin said. "Hurry! We gotta get through the Northeast Quadrant before dawn."

This caravan'll be a target in daylight.

At first there was grumbling, until women eight months

pregnant climbed out, then that humbled a few lazybones.

"Now push!" Crispin didn't know where the horses Charlie promised were, but they couldn't wait any longer. Shuli and a bunch more of the big guys were pulling with all their might. "We have to get out of here now!"

Finally, the carts began moving, but the sky was beginning to lighten.

What was it like in the other quadrant? Would there be opposition? Did they have enough weapons?

It was almost dawn when Charlie galloped up. "What happened to the horses?"

"I don't know, Charlie, they never got here."

"I told them to come straight here. Those fuckers. They went looting." Charlie got off his horse.

"No, Charlie, go get some horses for the carts. One's not going to do it. We need one for each cart. Thirty at least."

Charlie stopped. "You're right. I'll come back."

The bridge was in sight, and the men holding the bridge came running towards them, grabbing the carts, hauling them one by one to the bridge, and over.

Shuli moved like a man in a daze, and Crispin went over to him "You all right, buddy?"

"I'm beat, Crisp," Shuli said. "I don't think we're gonna make it."

"We'll make it," Crispin said. "Question is, what are we gonna do about them?"

Shuli looked ready to drop. "We gotta leave them. Maybe we can hide them somewhere and come back for them later."

Crispin didn't want to do that, but he didn't have much choice. A stand of trees lay just ahead and off the road. "Pull the carts over behind there," he said.

Pops was helping push the cart next to them and had heard everything. "You're gonna leave us?"

We're all exhausted.

Crispin sat on a big rock. He felt as bad as Shuli looked. "Eventually. Right now, let's get us somewhere safe, start a fire, get some rest."

***

Blocker woke up when the shooting started.

"They're here," Fish said. He'd decided they should stay up high, cut down guys as they approached. Except Fish wasn't all that good a shot.

"Save your ammo until they start shooting at us," Blocker said. The groups skulking about down there looked tired. "If they came from the fence they probably never walked this far in their life."

Fish laughed.

"Hey, Blocker, Fish." A guy stood in the doorway. "There's someone here to see you."

The guy outside their barricade looked ordinary enough, but he was on a horse. "You should all join us."

Blocker still had a sore throat, still felt tired, and it made him irritable. "Who the hell are you?"

"I'm from the Hartmanns. We're taking everything and leaving the city. Everyone's invited at the racetrack." He raised his voice. "Anyone want to get out of here, we'll get you a horse." He turned to Blocker. "We always invite people to join us before we loot them."

Blocker said, "We've been up all night. Can you give us some time to think about it?"

"Sure," he said. "Have breakfast even. We'll be back later for your answer." He galloped off.

"What an ass," Fish said. "I ain't going. The racetrack's out in the middle of nowhere."

Blocker felt the same way. "I'm going back to bed. Wake me up if he comes back."

It was late afternoon when Blocker woke up, and still the man hadn't come back.

Fish stood out in the middle of the street watching a big fire about three miles off which looked to be going the other way. There had been some fighting in neighboring areas. A few groups of ten or twelve men had arrived but kept going when they saw the barricades.

"They'll be back," Blocker said.

People began coming out when they saw him. "What will we do if the horse guy comes back?" a woman asked.

"Go if you want, but I'm not," said Fish. "This is my land. We got food, homes. I'd rather die than let some thug push me off my land."

A chorus of "Yeah" surrounded them.

"Guess we got our answer," the Hartmann guy yelled. "You heard 'em, men. Charge!"

Fifty horsemen came round the corner, leaped the barricade, and galloped towards them.

The people on the ground scattered to their houses.

The horses wheeled around, the leader saying something to the other men. They split up.

"Where the hell are they going?" Blocker said.

"I dunno," Fish said.

It was then the men came. Hundreds of men.

Dear gods, Blocker thought. *We're all going to die.*

***

After six hours sleep, some food, and bathing in the nearby river, Crispin almost felt human again. "Y'all stay here as long as you can. Don't bother with the bridge anymore; if anyone comes, just let them pass by. Stay hidden; we'll go get the horses. You got food, a fire, and water." It was still pretty cold at night, but they had plenty to wear. Pops and Nana would take care of them.

Pops stopped them. He had a huge blister on his foot, but he hobbled over. "It's a long way to the racetrack. You sure you wouldn't rather stay here?"

"I gotta find Charlie," Crispin said. "It's not like him to be gone this long. He might be hurt or something."

"I was thinking that too. You boys be careful."

Crispin, Shuli, and all the other men who could walk — about sixty of them — took the weapons and started off in a

115

cloudless late afternoon. The day was warm for March. The road here wasn't much more than dirt, but it was level. Where the hell were the horses? Where was Charlie?

"I have a bad feeling," Shuli said, "Charlie'd never leave us stuck out here."

Crispin nodded. "Yeah."

It was well past dark when a large group of horses came up. "Crispin Hartmann?"

"Over here," Crispin called out.

It was their men were riding. "Charlie needs you at the track," one man said, getting down off his horse. "We'll get the carts."

"Is he all right?"

"So far. He's been inviting people to join, and some real scary fellows showed up. Charlie's afraid if he leaves, he'll come back to find them in charge."

Charlie needs me, Crispin thought. He got on the horse. "I'll send more horses when I can," he told Shuli. "Be careful."

Shuli nodded. "I will."

It took Crispin three hours to get to the racetrack, and when he got there, he stopped in astonishment. The whole area in front of the complex was full of campfires! Hundreds of them!

Crispin picked his way along towards the racetrack, unchallenged until he got to the gates.

"Who goes there?"

A rush of fear: had the racetrack already been taken from them? "It's Crispin Hartmann. Charlie's brother. We run this place."

The man laughed, and his voice was familiar: his cousin Wànzi. "Damn, Crispin, thought I'd never see you again. Go on up, Charlie's waiting for you."

March 2nd

The men never stop, Blocker thought.

The Wheelcards used up all their ammo long ago. They were down to baseball bats, wooden boards, and knives. "We gotta get out of here."

"I'm not letting these fuckers take my land," Fish said. He'd been hit in the head, and now that's all he kept saying. Blocker was worried Fish wasn't thinking right anymore.

"What land?" Blocker heard women screaming from across the street through the open window. "If we don't get out of here now, there won't be any **us** left to hold it." A guy came in and got a bat to the face. "I'm getting out of here. Who's with me?"

Fish let out a crazy yell as he ran out and to the right.

"Gods, Fish, no!"

Fish got ten yards down the hall before he was cut down by gunshots.

"Goddamnit Fish! Why?"

His brother's body lay there.

How can I let him just lay there?

Blocker glanced back: eleven of them were left out of over a hundred. *We never should have tried to hold the neighborhood.* He put his hand on his forehead. *I got them into this; I gotta get them out.*

Blocker stared in anguish at his brother's body.

Gods, I'm sorry, Fish.

"Come on," Blocker said, and went the other way.

It took the group over an hour to sneak out of the neighborhood, and by that time, they had lost two and gained five. The men made their way to the river, their faces streaked with sweat, dirt, soot, and tears.

Blocker crouched behind a dock and surveyed the scene. Fires raged; men on horseback raced up and down. "We can't stay here," Blocker said. "Can all of you swim?"

"Goddamnit, Blocker," Turbo said, "I ain't swimming in that. We'll freeze to death."

"Then we gotta find a boat," Blocker said.

It was almost dark before they found enough boats for everyone. While they were looking, two women and three scared-looking kids joined them.

The women looked to be in bad shape, but they pulled the oars just as well as anyone, and the group made it to the Southwest Quadrant.

"We're the new Wheelcard Gang," Blocker said. "Let's find somewhere to sleep tonight."

March 3rd

Xavier found himself in a strange bed, his side wrapped. Every breath was agony.

"You're safe, son," Mr. Spadros said.

Xavier hurt too much to be dead. *This must be a hospital.* "What happened?"

Mr. Spadros held a crumpled note in his hand. "From your second. A man named Malize?"

Xavier nodded.

"Kerr found out about the attack somehow. He kidnapped his wife, told him he'd kill her if he didn't kill you first." He looked away.

Xavier took a painful breath. "One of your scientists must've told him."

"So you did get my message. Malize went along with his attack to lure Kerr's men out. Your men confirmed it — while you were briefing that last group, Malize told them what was happening, and what to do. He told them not to worry about hitting him."

Xavier let out a painful breath. *Could I have done the same in his shoes? Could I have stabbed one of my own men?*

If it was one of his men or one of his kids ....

Yes. But the thought gave him almost as much pain as his breathing did. "It seemed as if Ocho wanted to die, there at the end."

Mr. Spadros blinked. "He's not dead. Your men got to him in time. He's been in surgeries this whole time, but —"

"Truly? Oh, that's the best news I've heard all day."

"I haven't heard any news. The city — well, it's a shambles. Your children are safe. Jack wanted to come, but I wouldn't allow it."

"Good." Xavier didn't know what it was like out there, but it was no place for children. "Thank you for keeping them safe."

Mr. Spadros smiled, but Xavier could tell there was something he wasn't saying. "Did they get him?"

"Polansky Kerr got away," Mr. Spadros said, "him and most of his family. He set up a hot air balloon in the courtyard! The men finally shot it down as it sailed to the northeast, but I don't know if anyone survived the crash."

Hopefully we've seen the last of that man, Xavier thought, but something told him he hadn't.

Quint Varkonyi came in, handing a paper to Mr. Spadros. "The Cathedral, sir. It's fallen to the mob. Also, the Feds want to know if we require aid." He turned to Xavier. "Good to see you awake, sir."

The Cathedral? Xavier put his hand over his face. "Good gods. What have we done?"

Mr. Spadros sat heavily. "It's as my uncle said. Nothing will ever be the same." Mr. Spadros turned to Varkonyi, "Is there a way to help those women?"

Varkonyi shook his head. "Don't know how. It's every man for himself out there. The Guard is stretched to the breaking point defending the island as it is."

Mr. Spadros stood. "They promised to stop when we asked, and by the gods, they will stop!" He turned to Varkonyi. "Bring me Vincenzo Spadros."

After Varkonyi left, Xavier said, "Vincenzo Spadros ... the mobster?"

Mr. Spadros seemed uncomfortable. "Well, yes. My uncle." He let out a breath. "The Spadros Family paid for all this. I didn't want to have to take their help." He paused.

"But I suppose there have to be compromises made in order to get the job done."

So that's how he did it. "You sound quite the politician."

"No, I'm a schoolteacher." He frowned in disgust. "A schoolteacher who knows a group of undisciplined boys when he sees one." Mr. Spadros looked at the paper in his hand. "And I see the vultures, waiting to swoop down and seize our city while it lies bleeding. We can't survive without order, and order is what we shall have."

The Days Ahead

Acevedo learned many things during his time in the city. The Diamond clan barricaded the bridges to the Southwest Quadrant, including that to the island. They then released all the inmates in the Prison, offering them equal shares if they'd help loot the quadrant. The group seized the ray cannon from their rivals and killed Acevedo's brother Cavallo as he tried to escape. The cannon had been lost.

A group of indentured farmers in the Northeast Quadrant calling themselves The Clubbs of Justice seized the zeppelin station and the controls to the Aperture, refusing to let anyone in or out of the city until their rambling set of demands were met. Acevedo wasn't sure they even knew what they wanted.

While it meant no one could bring in supplies or reinforcements, it also meant Polansky Kerr wouldn't be able to escape the city. The "Clubbs" (they insisted on the spelling) hated the Kerrs, blaming them for the mistreatment they received at the hands of their masters.

A large group calling themselves the Hartmanns — who seemed to grow in numbers as time passed — pillaged much of the city, settling around the racetrack. They had begun building homes near the track, the whole group coming together to build each one, and were managing to build two or three a week.

Although they had sacked the Cathedral, their leader, the big red-haired man from the meeting, said it was done wrongly, without orders from him. "If you see anyone calling themselves Hartmanns, you know they aren't with us," the man said. "We're the Harts now." He insisted on that spelling as well.

The new Director of the Dealers, a woman named Octavia Underlead, came to Acevedo. She refused to have anything to do with rebuilding the city, and asked him not to touch the Cathedral. "Director Deschapelles and twenty-three Dealers died defending our right to protect Bridges. Please honor her last wishes in this."

Acevedo didn't understand.

"The knowledge we bear is for the King and the Dealers alone," she said. "You are neither. The calculations, signs, and divinations are clear: the city will endure a hundred years. When the city is in great need, when the woman is provided and the land restored, the Dealers will return. Until then, we stay outside with our people."

Acevedo didn't understand that either. Surely the city was in great need now.

But he had never been a religious man.

***

To maintain a show of a stable government for the Feds, Acevedo persuaded Xavier to be sworn in as the first Mayor of Bridges as soon as he was well enough to stand.

A week later, moving under heavy guard, Acevedo brought Xavier to collect his children and bring them to the island, where they would be safer.

He'll do better with his children near him, Acevedo thought.

***

Xavier stared out of the carriage window the entire trip, appalled at the sights he saw along the way, and by the time they got to the building, he felt shaken.

But when he saw his children, he ran to them. Jack and Joy threw themselves into their father's arms, and Xavier didn't even care how much his side hurt. "You're safe, you're safe," Xavier felt closer to tears than he'd been in a long time.

***

Acevedo was pleased to see his brothers standing guard around the building, and he went to greet each of them in turn. He felt acutely aware of Cavallo's loss, even more so when he saw Cavallo's son Roman and his new wife.

"I'm so sorry," Acevedo said as he hugged them. "Your Papa loved you both very much."

"I know," Roman said. "We've decided if this is a boy, to name him Cavallo."

Acevedo smiled. "I'm sure he would like that."

***

Xavier was surprised to see his father also was there. "I came as soon as I heard you were hurt, but with the station closed, it was only now I could get here."

Xavier put his hand on his father's shoulder. "I'm glad you're back."

Jack looked up at them. "I asked Molly Bluff's mother if I could court her. She said yes."

"Oh?" Xavier said.

"Well, if I can get a surgeon apprenticeship. I want to be able to support her."

Xavier smiled. *He's so much like I was at that age.*

Once Xavier got it in his mind to marry their mother,

nothing would stop him. Gaining a proper station in order to marry was why he joined the Guard in the first place. "Then I approve."

***

A hand on Acevedo's shoulder: he turned, and Katherine stood behind him.

Acevedo turned, taking her hand. "There you are. There's something I've been meaning to ask you."

"Yes."

Acevedo blinked, confused. "I didn't ask anything yet."

Katherine took hold of his upper arms. "I don't care. Whatever you ask, the answer is yes."

"Are you saying —?"

She smiled. "Yes."

Overwhelmed, Acevedo kissed her right there in front of everyone, not caring what anyone thought.

After a moment, he felt Molly's eyes on him."I suppose this means you're going to be my father now?"

Acevedo smiled, and took her hand. "Yes, my dear, I think it does."

***

It took a while for Xavier to feel as if something terrible wasn't going to happen at any minute.

Mr. Spadros came to him, a cup in hand. "You look like you need more pain medicine."

Xavier nodded, took the draught, went to sit by his father. "I feel like I can't relax."

His father nodded. "Too much happened to you. It takes a while to get used to being safe again. Like getting your land legs after being on the river all day."

Xavier laughed. "Yeah. Like that!" He studied his father's face. "But it goes away?"

His father shrugged. "Most times."

"Dad, I'm sorry. I didn't understand how it was for you."

His dad put a hand on his knee. "It's all right, son. Maybe now things will go better for all of us."

Later at dinner, Jack said, "Are you really Mayor of Bridges now?"

"I am."

Jack pondered that a long time. "I'm proud of you for what you did. Molly told me what it was like out there in the tent camps —"

*When was **she** out there?*

"— and it would've been wrong to let the King kill all those people. You had to do something."

This made Xavier feel better than it reasonably should have. Since his wife died, his children had been everything to him. And now, they were growing up. "I'm proud of you too, Jack."

***

Many of the parents, after hearing of what happened in the city, decided to stay at the science building until the situation was more settled. Clothing and food had been brought for them, and they began dividing the tasks and clearing out rooms to stay in.

"You'll have a place with the Spadros Family as long as you stay here," Acevedo told them. "This isn't over yet."

Bandits had tried to take the building once already while he had been gone, but were repelled by the parents and students. The countryside was in an uproar, and when they heard the Mayor was there, delegations came to express their displeasure for a week straight.

Xavier often seemed unsure as to how to proceed. "Pretend they're your men," Acevedo said. "Or think of what old King Taylor might do. You can handle this."

Each time, Xavier would nod, then talk to the people, remind them they could handle the bandits, and they would go away satisfied.

Then it was time for Xavier to return home. "I'll go with you," Acevedo said.

"Molly and I will come as well," Katherine said.

Acevedo went to her. "It's very dangerous still. Do you think this wise?"

Katherine said. "I just recalled a certain evening —"

Instantly, Acevedo knew which one.

"— and I think it would be better for me to live on the island, at least until our wedding."

Acevedo grinned. "Very well. All the more reason for me to escort you."

Those returning to the city got into the carriages.

Xavier was going to get in with his children and Molly, who sat next to Jack, but then stopped. "I must speak with Mr. Spadros."

"I'll go with them," his father said. "I want to spend more time with my grandchildren."

Xavier grinned. The fact that his father had come back at all was encouraging. "Very good."

Xavier went forward to the carriage and got in, followed by Mr. Spadros. Mrs. Bluff and Trapasso Spadros sat there already. The doors closed and the carriages set off.

Xavier said, "What exactly does a Mayor do?"

Mr. Spadros said, "Leads the city, I guess."

"I want you to find out. From history."

Mr. Spadros laughed. "Very well. I suppose I'll be personal librarian to the Mayor now."

Xavier grinned. Mr. Spadros did look like one.

Then they began talking of other things. Mr. Spadros mentioned the Harts, and how they had changed their name, and Trapasso Spadros laughed. "They're trying to become legitimate," he said. "We never had to change our name. We just had you, Acevedo."

Mr. Spadros seemed unsure as to what to think of that.

A sound as if a gun being fired came from his right, then a horrifying high squealing whistle. A crash of splintering wood as the ground shook. The carriage lifted in the air and set down, almost tipping.

What just happened? Xavier got out and looked around.

Burning pieces of a carriage lay everywhere. Horses lay on the ground. Guardsmen on horses milled around, began dismounting.

Mrs. Bluff screamed and ran over, along with several of the parents, who began beating the flames with their coats.

Terror struck. Xavier rushed forward. "My children are in there!"

Mr. Spadros grabbed him, yelling, "Stop. Stop!"

Xavier pulled away, ran over, frantic.

Men pulled a charred body out.

Xavier's vision turned gray, his knees buckled, his stomach roiled.

Mr. Spadros knelt by him, grasping his upper arms.

"Kerr did this," Xavier said. "Polansky Kerr. He told me if I did anything, he'd kill them. And he did. He did."

People from the ruins began gathering. One yelled, "It's them! You did this! You destroyed my city!"

More and more angry people came out of the burnt buildings and makeshift tents which used to be the "Pot of Gold." Some carried boards, others pieces of metal. Rocks and broken bottles began to fly towards the Guardsmen.

"Protect the Mayor," Mr. Spadros yelled. "Get the bodies and let's go!"

Xavier couldn't move.

Bodies. Jack and Joy — my children — are bodies?

A group of Xavier's men lifted him into the carriage, then began shooting into the crowd. A few from other carriages climbed in as well.

Mr. Spadros said, "Where's Katherine?"

"With Molly," a woman said. "They're bringing her straight to the hospital."

Mr. Spadros said. "Molly's alive?"

"Yes," a man said. "She's hurt, but she's alive."

"Polansky Kerr said he would kill them," Xavier said.

Then he realized: *The rocket was also meant for me.*

Mr. Spadros said, "Yes. I know."

"I'm going to kill him," Xavier said.

Mr. Spadros sat looking at him for a long time. Then he said, "Do you want help?"

Xavier thought of his men. "No," he said. "I have all the help I need."

They went to Market Center in silence. When they got out of the carriages, Xavier said, "Get my top men."

The men who would do anything for him came round. "I have one final mission for you."

When he told them what it was, they grinned in delight.

***

On October 17th, six months and sixteen days after the fighting began, Xavier Alcatraz gave his first speech as Mayor of Bridges.

He went to the podium, looked out over the crowd.

"Our long night of unspeakable tragedy is finally over."

Then he stepped down, overcome. The speech he had written seemed useless.

My children are dead. My father is dead. My city is ruined.

Xavier felt ruined as well. People were already calling this the Alcatraz Coup.

I'll be named a cheat and a traitor until the day I die.

The crowd was silent for a long moment. Then they burst into applause.

Xavier just wanted to go somewhere and hide for the rest of his life. But there were delegations to meet with, orders to sign. At least the looting had finally stopped; the city was more or less at peace.

Ocho Malize and his wife sat in the audience, holding their new baby.

The doctors said Ocho would never walk again.

But they named their new baby Xavier.

Xavier would make sure they were taken care of.

He glanced over at Mr. Spadros and Mrs. Bluff; they stood holding hands.

Xavier didn't know Mrs. Bluff well, but he felt grateful her daughter Molly would live. Jack had loved her, if only for a little while. And Mrs. Bluff had helped him with Joy when no one else would; for that he was grateful.

They seemed good together.

At least someone in all this is happy.

Xavier looked out over the ruins of Bridges. His city was free. But at what cost?

He took a deep breath, let it out. Jack and Joy would want him to go on. So somehow, he would.

There was a lot to do still. His work had only begun.

Molly Bluff was thrown from the carriage in the rocket attack on the Mayor's convoy. She lost her right arm after it was crushed by one of the fallen horses. Molly joined the Dealers two years later, where she remained until her death at the age of 47.

One year after the Coup, Xavier's men located Polansky Kerr. Once the heads of the Kerr family were displayed on pikes at the four bridges to Market Center, most believed that the Kerr Dynasty was destroyed.

Xavier Alcatraz was mayor of Bridges for thirty-six years. He was assassinated just days before his 68th birthday. The culprit was never found.

Acevedo Spadros married Katherine Bluff. Under his rule, the Spadros crime family expanded its influence over much of the city. Acevedo died two years after Xavier, convinced that one of the Kerrs still lived and was responsible for Xavier's death.

The Pot of Gold was never rebuilt.

Genealogy

Trapasso Spadros
Nina
Katherine Bluff
Acevedo Spadros
Cavallo Spadros
Roman Spadros
Liza Spadros
Cavallo Roman Spadros
Acevedo Spadros II
Roy Spadros

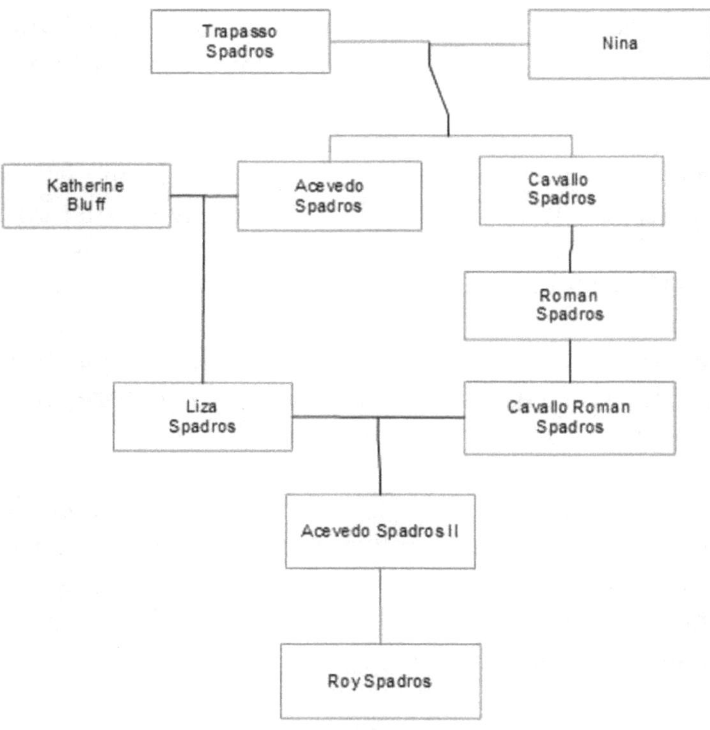

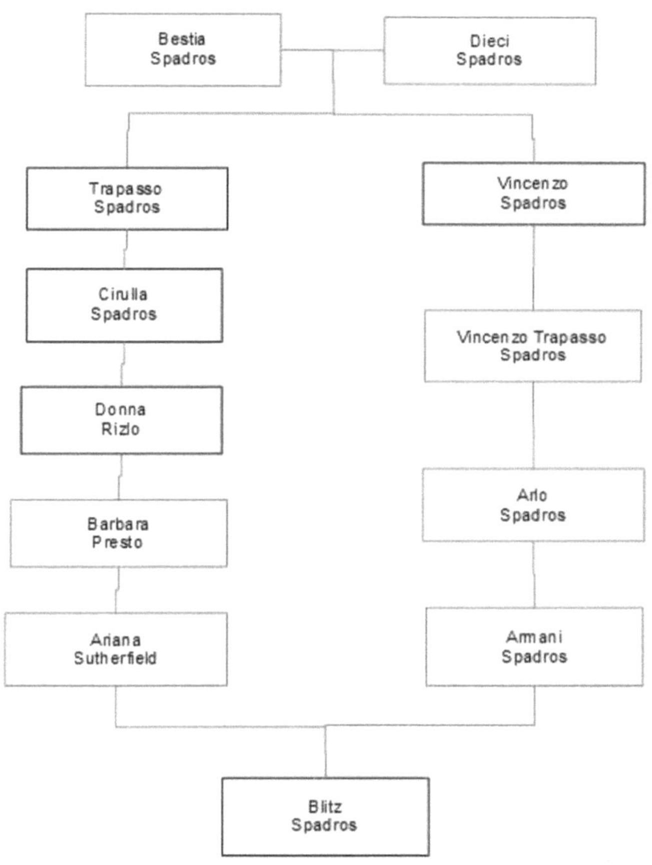

Bestia
Spadros

Dieci
Spadros

Trapasso
Spadros

Vincenzo
Spadros

Cirulla
Spadros

Vincenzo Trapasso
Spadros

Donna
Rizlo

Arlo
Spadros

Barbara
Presto

Ariana
Sutherfield

Armani
Spadros

Blitz
Spadros

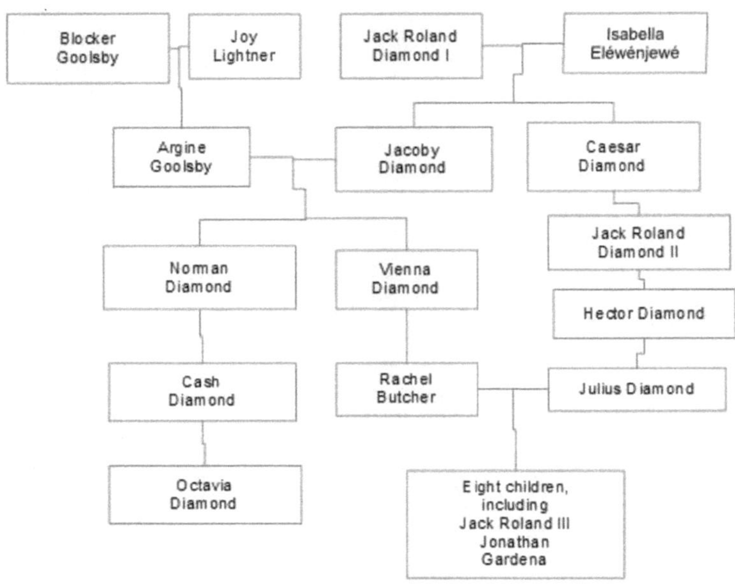

Blocker Goolsby
Joy Lightner
Jack Roland Diamond I
Isabella Eléwénjewé
Argine Goolsby
Jacoby Diamond
Caesar Diamond
Norman Diamond
Vienna Diamond
Jack Roland Diamond II
Hector Diamond
Cash Diamond
Rachel Butcher
Julius Diamond
Octavia Diamond
Eight children, including Jack Roland III Jonathan Gardena

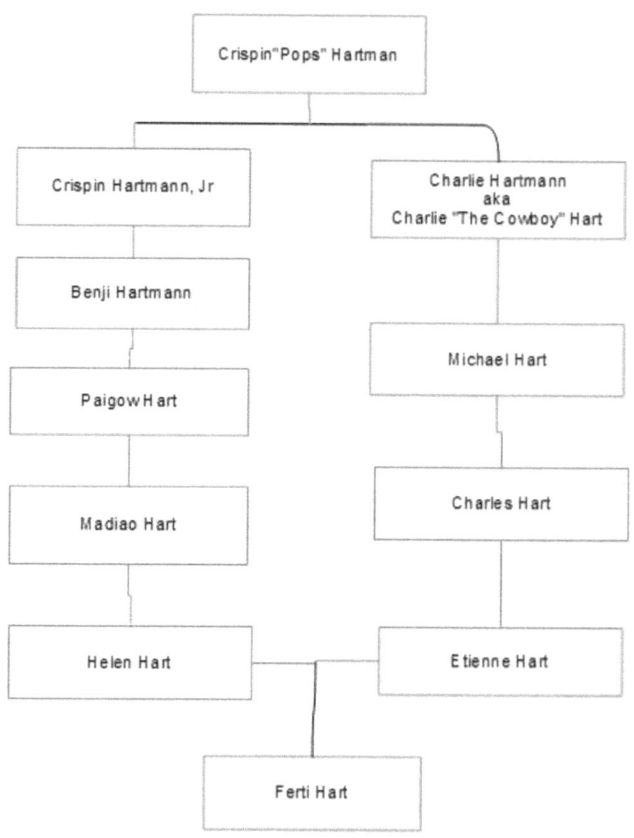

Crispin "Pops" Hartman
Crispin Hartmann, Jr
Charlie Hartmann
aka
Charlie "The Cowboy" Hart
Benji Hartmann
Michael Hart
Paigow Hart
Charles Hart
Madiao Hart
Helen Hart
Etienne Hart
Ferti Hart

About the Author

Patricia Loofbourrow is a writer, gardener, artist, musician, poet, wildcrafter, and married mother of three who loves power tools, dancing, genetics, and anything to do with outer space.

She also has an M.D. Heinlein would be proud.

Acknowledgements

So many people have helped bring you this story. I'd like to thank Corwin Loofbourrow for his developmental and beta-reader input, Erin Hartshorn for dropping everything (twice!) to help with proofreading and formatting, and Anita Carroll for her cover design.

If it were not for the tireless work done by my street team, The Commission, this book might never have made it into your hands.

I want to give special thanks to my Patrons for their generous monthly support of my work:

Dave Kobrenski

Cristina

Nancy

Phoebe Darqueling

Eirlys Evans

To become a Patron, subscribe on my Patreon page!
Patreon.com/red_dog_conspiracy

The Alcatraz Coup is a prequel
set 100 years before the steampunk neo-noir series
the **Red Dog Conspiracy**

The Jacq of Spades:
Part 1 of the **Red Dog Conspiracy**
Available through most reputable book-sellers
In Hardcover, paperback, e-reader, and audio formats

The once-beautiful domed neo-Victorian city of Bridges is split between four crime families in an uneasy cease-fire. Social disparity increasing and its steam-driven infrastructure failing, a new faction is on the rise: the Red Dogs.

Jacqueline Spadros has a dream life: a wealthy husband, a powerful family. But her life is not what it seems. Kidnapped from her mother's brothel and forced to marry, the murder of her best friend Air ten years before haunts her nightmares. She finds moments of freedom in a small-time private eye business, which she hides in fear of her sadistic father-in-law.

Air's little brother disappears off his back porch and the Red Dogs are framed for it. With the help of a mysterious gentleman investigator hired by the Red Dogs to learn the truth, Jacqui pushes her abilities to their limits in hope of rescuing the child before the kidnapper disposes of him.

A preview of *The Jacq of Spades*:

The Letter

A domed city, split by four rivers, an island at its center. In the southeast quadrant, a taxi-carriage pulled up to a shop on 2nd Street. In the gutter lay a card:

BRIDGES: 500 YEARS OF CULTURE

THE JEWEL OF THE GREAT PLAINS

The postcard depicting an elegant couple crossing a golden bridge lay in horse manure. A carriage-track ran through it.

I stepped over the scene as I climbed from the taxi-carriage, my borrowed boots grating on the rough concrete sidewalk. Trash flew past in the wind. The air smelled of rain, clouds hanging dark in the afternoon sky. "How much to wait?"

The clocks chimed half past two. The driver, in his sixties, pushed his goggles up on his forehead. His horse tossed its head and shifted. "Here? Penny now, penny when you done," he paused, leering, "cause I like you." He made no attempt to hide his survey of my person.

Unimpressed, I handed him the penny, entering the white wooden storefront as large drops fell.

The floorboards squeaked. The front room, lit by a bulb hanging from the ceiling, smelled of mildew. Grayish-green paint flaked off the walls.

The woman behind the counter, pale with graying brown hair, wore widow's brown. "Welcome to Bryce Fabrics. How can I help you?"

Eleanora. When I last saw her ten years ago, she screamed curses and wept. How could she be here? What would she do? I felt an urge to run.

I took a deep breath. A child changed more in ten years than a woman. Her face held no recognition. "You sent for assistance?"

"Oh! Yes!" She grabbed my hand, her relief plain. "I'm Eleanora Bryce. I'm so glad you came."

She led me behind the counter and into their back room. Three beds and a rickety desk lined the walls. A small table with two stools sat in the center. A rusty hat-rack stood in the corner close by: three thin, battered coats hung there.

A tall, thin adolescent with dark hair sat on a stool in the far left corner. He pointed when I entered the room. "That's her!"

He was six when last I saw him. How did he recognize me?

He held up the newspaper with my portrait (among others) on the front page. Emblazoned across the top, it read:

GRAND BALL EXTRAVAGANZA

Bridges Family Meeting Countdown

Mrs. Bryce grabbed the paper from his hand, then peered at me. "Herbert, you're right, it is her!"

Mrs. Bryce appeared astonished to see me in my disguise: a shop maid's uniform, black with a white apron. "Mrs. Spadros herself!" She curtsied. "I would never have called if I would have known such a fine lady would answer!"

I felt sad. Would she be glad to see me if she learned my true identity? Would she curtsy then, or would she strike me?

Rain beat against the windows and lightning flashed, the rumbling of thunder close behind.

Herbert didn't bow.
Those same eyes.
The same pale serious face.

"Jacqui, don't go."
The moon hung high overhead. The frigid air smelled of dirt and sweat. Thirty children trained at knife-fighting by lamp-light a few yards up the narrow alley. "Please don't go. This feels bad. Men don't want little kids for nothing good."

Mrs. Bryce said, "My boy's gone missing."
Startled at her words, I jolted out of the memory. "What?"
"My son. He's missing. It's why I called you." Several portraits sat upon a tiny dresser in the corner across the room to the right. Mrs. Bryce went to it and handed me a tintype photo: a boy. Light skin, dark hair, dark eyes, round face. She claimed he was twelve; he looked closer to ten.

Sitting with Ma at her trestle table in the cathedral, eating warm bread with butter. The sounds of moaning and panting down the hall behind the tan linen curtains. Telling Ma our story and laughing at escaping the police. The smells of sex and baking in the air. His big dark eyes happy, his pale face flushed with the liquor he tasted and the candle-lit warmth. His little legs kicked under the stool ...

I shook my head, trying to clear the memories of that terrible night. "This is a recent picture?"
Mrs. Bryce nodded. "Yes, mum, taken before Yuletide. Maybe three weeks ago? Right after we moved here."
"And you're sure he didn't run off?"
Mrs. Bryce's brown eyes filled with tears. "No, mum, I swear. David was a good boy, in the midst of his chore-work. 'Off to sweep the stair,' he said, 'I'll be right back.' He never came in."

Thunder pealed. Harsh light illuminated the barren room.

I called myself an investigator, but I investigated minor matters: a missing dog, renters who moved without paying. So this case violated rules I laid for myself. I avoided police affairs …

"I can't pay you …" Mrs. Bryce said.

… and I didn't do a case without payment in advance. Not even this one.

"… but I'll do whatever you like, anything, if you'll help me."

I never liked Eleanora. She never liked me. When she realized who I was ….

"Please, mum, I know how it looks. The police said he run off, but I know he was taken and they all ignore me."

This woman lived most of her life a dozen blocks from this very point, well on the other side of that spiked wrought-iron fence encircling the Pot. Why would she expect the police to help an out-of-town widow with no Family connections and no bribe money? Had she really forgotten?

My borrowed corset pinched at the hips; it chafed with every move. I wanted to change into my own clothes, get away from this room full of bad memories and guilt.

I regarded the portrait, feeling melancholy: David looked just like him. "Show me where you last saw the boy."

The Bryce's back stair appeared much like any two blocks from the Pot: rickety wooden steps with rusty metal banisters leading down to a rat-infested alley.

Clouds loomed dark across the sky. The only real light came from an oil lamp far down the alley to our right. We took refuge from the downpour under the eaves, out of the wind.

A dark figure moved in the shadows twenty yards to our left. Something about him frightened me. I hoped the rain would hide our words and send him away.

"When your boy disappeared, did you find anything amiss?"

"Everything was as it should be, except I found his little

broom on the ground," her voice broke, "and him gone."

I surveyed the alley. It appeared normal ... except ...

I crossed towards a red spot on the far wall, near waist level. "Was this here before he went missing?"

"No, mum, at least, I don't think so."

I leaned over to examine the spot, Tenni's corset stabbing at my midsection. A solid red silhouette of a dog, ink-stamped onto the wall.

The tower clock chimed three. The man began walking towards us.

"I must go." I might be Jacqueline Spadros, but that would hardly stop a scoundrel from committing robbery or worse before he learned of it. We hurried back inside, and I breathed a sigh of relief when the door locked behind me.

Then I remembered I carried weapons, and felt silly.

Mrs. Bryce said, "You're going to find him ... right?"

I shook my head and kept walking through the room. The situation frightened me. "This is a police matter, and I can't be involved. No quadrant-lady can, but especially not me."

"But—"

I turned to her. "Do you realize who my father-in-law is? What he would do to all three of us (I gestured at Herbert) if he learned I came here?"

She turned even paler than she was, and nodded.

"Don't ever contact me at my home again. It's much too dangerous. If you wish to hire me in the future, send a note to Madame Biltcliffe. Address it to my maid Amelia Dewey."

Mrs. Bryce stared at me, mouth open. "I — I never sent anything to your home, mum! I swear!"

I put my hand in my pocket, touched the letter hidden there. "I'm curious. Why did you contact Madame Biltcliffe?" My dressmaker Marie Biltcliffe owned a shop in downtown Spadros quadrant; she sent me cases from time to time.

"When I went to the police station, mum," she said, "a couple sat nearby. They must have heard me talk to the constable. The lady told me I might find help there."

A couple so certain of Madame Biltcliffe's association with an investigator that they told others of it? "Did they give names?"

"I didn't ask," Mrs. Bryce said. "I was so upset ..."

"I understand. What did the couple look like?"

Mrs. Bryce smiled like a young girl. "Nice looking, especially the man!" She fanned herself with her left hand. "They were about your age, and the lady had red hair."

This didn't help much. "If you meet them again, please let me know." I felt like a traitor. "I'm sorry, I really am. But I can't help you. Leave this to the police."

Walking through the front room of this shop, I knew the right thing to do, even then. But I felt too afraid.

I handed the taxi-driver his penny. "Madame Biltcliffe's dress shop on 42nd street, please."

His mother Eleanora, in Bridges, her youngest gone missing.

David looked just like him.

"Jacqui, you shouldn't go."

Heedless of the pedestrians and carriages beside me in the street, I wept.

I entered Madame Biltcliffe's dress shop through her back door. A warm glow and the smell of fresh linen greeted me. Madame's shop maid Tenni handed me a hat box. "For tonight."

I smiled. Quite clever, Madame.

Tenni was just seventeen, yet appeared much like me from behind — curled reddish-brown hair, light brown skin. We wore close to the same size, and I often used Tenni as a decoy when on a case: I would wear her clothes, and she mine.

We went to a fitting room. Tenni helped me change into my original dress, a peacock blue walking gown. My husband Tony said he liked it because it matched my eyes.

I sighed with relief on removing Tenni's new maid's corset, which left a red mark on my hip. "Did anyone inquire for me?"

"No, mum. And I stayed out of sight, as you asked."

"Good girl." I gave her a penny.

Tenni curtsied. "Thank you, mum."

"Ask Madame to return."

Madame Marie Biltcliffe entered: a tall, handsome, middle-aged woman with perfect black hair.

"Have either of you spoken to anyone about my business? Someone who decided not to contact me?"

They both shook their heads.

"I have never had anyone refuse your help who I referred," Madame said. "And I never speak your name before the meeting."

"Mrs. Bryce said a young woman with red hair told her to contact you."

Madame Biltcliffe frowned. "I know of no such woman."

"I feel confused, Madame. When Mrs. Bryce wrote you, why did you not contact me?"

She seemed surprised. "I never contact you until I speak with the woman myself. I didn't know her, and she merely sent a note. If she would have waited —"

I shook my head. "She says she didn't write to me."

"How strange." Madame Biltcliffe appeared as perplexed as I felt. "I suppose I am glad she is no forger."

I laughed at that thought. "No, that she is not."

I remembered my sore midsection. "Would you make a maid's corset for me to keep here for future use?"

"I would be happy to." Madame Biltcliffe smiled and went to the curtain, holding it open for me. I emerged from the dressing room, and she curtsied as I passed by.

I breezed out of the shop and onto the street. My black and silver carriage stood ready, drawn by black horses with silver tackle. As I took my day footman Skip Honor's hand to enter the coach, I glanced to my left.

A man wearing brown stood several doors down, turning away at my glance. I didn't see his face, but he seemed familiar. I felt certain he had been watching me.

I turned to Honor. "That man. How long has he stood there?"

But when Honor and I looked again, the man was gone.

While in the coach on the way home, I pulled the letter from my pocket.

> Dear Mrs. Spadros —
>
> I hate to impose upon you during the holiday, but it would be of much help if you could find time to call on me today. My maid Tenni will, of course, be ready to assist you. It is a matter of some urgency.
>
> Your servant, Marie Biltcliffe

The letter, on Madame's stationery, scented with her perfume, in her handwriting. Madame claimed she never sent it. Mrs. Bryce claimed she never sent it either. Then who did?

A puzzle. I moved the pieces around in my mind and could make nothing of it.

***

I hope you've enjoyed this preview.
Visit JacqOfSpades.com
To learn more about this best selling series
Over 23,000 copies sold!